The sharks were not ~~ dards, but plenty large. ~~ feet long. Twenty feet ~~ sudden, spasmodic downward jerk, one of the sharks snatched a dwarf from his seat and bit him in two.

The legs, still kicking, floated down trailing a cloud of blood. The crowd shrieked. Those nearest panicked but those sitting farther away loved it. Neptune laughed his mad laugh, and the laugh was echoed from every wet corner of the colosseum.

Neptune and his boys were just as suddenly back on the other side of the wall, back in their comfortable seats, settling in for the spectacle of slaughter.

"They can't get out, can they?" Christopher wailed.

"Great Athena save us!" Nikos cried.

The nearest shark swam right up to the barrier separating water and air. Then it kept swimming. As its snout emerged, a water bubble formed, encasing the beast.

The shark, within its undulating bubble, swam floating through the air. Mouth open now. Rows and rows of serrated triangular teeth.

Straight for us . . .

Look for other EVERWORLD titles

by K.A. Applegate:

EVER WORLD

UNDERSTAND THE UNKNOWN

K.A. APPLEGATE

SCHOLASTIC INC.
New York Toronto London Auckland Sydney
Mexico City New Delhi Hong Kong

No part of this publication may be reproduced in whole or in part, or stored in a retrieval system, or transmitted in any form or by any means, electronic, mechanical, photocopying, recording, or otherwise, without written permission of the publisher. For information regarding permission, write to Scholastic Inc., Attention: Permissions Department, 555 Broadway, New York, NY 10012.

ISBN 0-590-87986-3

12 11 10 9 8 7 6 5 4   1 2 3 4 5/0

Printed in the U.S.A.

First Scholastic printing, November 2000

THE AUTHOR WISHES TO THANK ELISE SMITH FOR HER HELP IN PREPARING THIS MANUSCRIPT.

FOR MICHAEL AND JAKE

UNDERSTAND THE UNKNOWN

There's a saying: It was the calm before the
storm. Maybe it originated with people who
lived close to the water and learned to read its
rhythms and moods. Maybe those people had to
get smart enough to read the world around
them, the changing wind and air pressure and
light, in order to predict what was going to happen next. In order to survive.

Maybe some poet first said it just that way, "It
was the calm before the storm," talking about
how once disaster hits, people tend to look back
and remember just how peaceful everything
seemed before. Even if, in reality, things were
never really calm.

Anyway, it was the calm before the storm.
Again. Because in Everworld, there's pretty much

always a storm just waiting to crash down on your head. The calm is never more than temporary.

We were five teenagers from the Chicago area and we were a long, long way from the peaceful shores of Lake Michigan. We had just left a shattered, bloody Egypt and its musty, moribund gods. We were hoping to get back to Mount Olympus, where we would help its ranting, juvenile gods destroy the Hetwan, the forces of the alien god-eating god, Ka Anor. And we were traveling in a quinquireme, a Roman adaptation of a Greek or Carthaginian trireme. The crew was Greek. The captain was a small, dark man named Nikos.

How had a Roman warship manned by a Greek crew gotten to Egypt? Why was a warship being used to carry a cargo of dates, palm oil, and dried fish? I didn't even bother to ask. There was probably some sort of explanation, magical or otherwise, but I'd long ago stopped needing to know the "why." I just dealt with the facts. There was a ship with a crew and the captain was willing to sail us down the Nile, out of Egypt, and into the ocean or sea or whatever the hell it was out there. We'd paid him off in gold looted from the temple of Isis. Isis didn't need it.

Around me the others slept. April, Christopher, Jalil. Only Senna was fully awake, sitting with her knees to her chest, gazing at the blue sky. I was tired, too, but didn't feel like sleeping. Didn't want to go to sleep and cross over to the real world, the old world. Just wasn't in the mood to deal with my mother or my job or school or any of those other people and things about my old life that no longer seemed very important.

Nikos had let me take the rudder once I'd demonstrated that I was no lubber. So I stood in the stern, working the large oar that hung over the port side, observing the sky, the sea, excited in spite of myself to be on this ship. The quinquereme — a ship I never imagined seeing — was a long and slender warship. She was more a galley than a sailboat, really. The single rectangular sail was really of use only when the wind came from right astern and now with the wind on our starboard quarter, the sail was furled.

The boat had oars on each side, set in banks of five. There were three levels of benches, with two rowers on the top bench per side, two in the middle level, and one strong rower on each side of each bottom bench. As with the Viking longboat, the crew had to row in unison or they'd foul one anothers' oars. But in this case the ship carried less than a third of its nominal crew, so the oars were plied with less discipline and the ship moved sluggishly.

Back in the real world, I'd been doing some reading on great societies, particularly those that had risen and prospered through warfare of one sort or another. The real world was still good for that: for books. And the Romans made good reading.

The Romans were professional borrowers. Copycats and mimics. In typical fashion the Romans had stolen the idea for the quinquireme from the Greeks and improved on it. It was a cool ship, with its painted eyes on the bow and the long, dangerous ram that protruded underwater. It was a state-of-the-art killing machine, the Everworld equivalent of an Aegis class cruiser. Of course, if it had been relegated to merchant shipping and/or smuggling, it had to be on its last legs.

But old and tired, or fresh out of the shipyard, it was pretty much the same ship I'd have seen two thousand years ago in the real Rome, in the ancient real world. The real world had moved on, the real world had learned how to design sails and yards and masts and above all true rudders to allow a boat to lie close to the wind. Everworld had stagnated.

I could build a boat that would sail rings around anything anyone here had. As mighty as this ship was in its heyday, I nevertheless could take some weekend sailor's twenty-eight-footer and a box of Molotov cocktails and sink this ship or anything the Romans or the Greeks could float.

Still and all, it was a cool boat.

I glanced again at Senna, apart and alone. At April, curled into the fetal position, her long red hair covering her face like a blanket. At Christopher, head leaning back against the side of the ship, mouth open, snoring. At Jalil, sitting a few feet from where Christopher sprawled, arms folded across his chest, head down, long legs straight out in front of him.

Who were these people, really?

I'm not good at people and their motivations, what makes them tick and why. It's a serious weakness. I usually don't get people right, not at first anyway. Still, you can't spend days and days and what might be months, for all I know — the passing of time in Everworld having little if anything to do with the passing of time in the real world — with the same people without knowing something about them. Without coming to some sort of conclusion about their personalities and characters. Without knowing, or being able to make a pretty close guess, what they might do or say in a particular situation.

Jalil is smart and unsentimental. Intellectually unsentimental, I mean; he doesn't shade or dilute the truth: He takes it straight up. I admire that. But it means that sometimes he's with me, sometimes not. I trust him as a person, but he's no friend of mine, not really. There's no ordering Jalil to do something, no cajoling him, either. You convince Jalil. There's no other way to move him.

He and Senna have a strange relationship, maybe as strange as my own with her. I don't understand the nature of their connection, don't know where or when the roots were put down. But I do know, or think I do, that after what happened in Africa with the Orisha, after I agreed to help Jalil use Senna — use her for the good of the group — after that, Senna wanted very badly to hurt Jalil. Maybe not kill him, because I'm pretty sure that each of us is still of some use to Senna and her own personal goals. But maybe make Jalil wish he were dead.

April is Senna's half sister and everything

Senna is not. She's honest. She actually cares about other people. She's no cynic. She's pretty and sexy and dramatic and funny. She's the girl you want to go out with because you know you'll have fun and you know things won't get weird and you know that even if it doesn't work out she'll let you down gently.

Senna, on the other hand, is the girl you want to go out with for the same reason you want to ride a Harley without a helmet.

It's fair to say that April loathes Senna, and though I can point to more than a few reasons for April to be angry at Senna, I just don't get the depth of the loathing. But, like I said, I don't get a lot of things. And as long as I can keep those two from killing each other, I guess I'll have done my job.

Christopher is a tough case to figure, though. Since this craziness started he's changed some. Christopher's always been right out there, totally up front about who he is, what he is — weak or strong, a jerk or a clown or a stand-up guy. When he's an a-hole, he's an unapologetic a-hole. When he's brave (and he often is) he still bitches about it. The whole stoic, take-it-like-a-man thing is lost on Christopher.

He drinks. My opinion? He drinks too much.

Maybe he's an alcoholic, I don't know. Maybe he'll beat it. He seems to be getting past his more outrageous racial stuff at least. That's progress, so maybe Christopher will get it together in the end.

Senna. What can I say about Senna; what can anyone say? Human but other. Witch — but good or bad or a little of both? I suspect that only Senna knows who or what Senna really is. And I suspect she wants it that way.

There was a time when I needed, when I wanted Senna. There was a time when I was the addict and she was my pipe. I'm past that. As past it as any junkie ever is. Back in Egypt, finally, after almost ten years apart, Senna came face-to-face with her mother. Not a happy reunion. Not exactly an Oprah moment.

Her mother is a self-serving creature, not so different from Senna herself, though without her daughter's genius for cool, deliberate manipulation. Senna's mom had abandoned her, basically to save her own ass and have what she thought would be a better life. Senna was not forgiving. Senna has what you might call flexible morals: Whatever she does to other people is fine; what anyone does to her is unforgivable.

Not exactly an earthshaking surprise to me.

And anyway, not my problem. I tried to turn my mind to the tactical position back at Olympus. That was our goal.

The Hetwan were besieging the mountain but had been stopped. For now. We had done a deal with the Coo-Hatch that should keep them from providing their primitive cannon to the Hetwan. Should. And the Greek defenses around Olympus should hold now. Should.

I tried to think about all that, tried to play Napoleon, to see the way to win. But I had a steering oar in my hand and tucked under my arm, and I felt the living deck of the ship under my feet, and I heard the creak and splash of the oars and the steady music of water rushing along the hull, and my mind was seduced away by those basic pleasures. I love boats.

I let go of worry and figured to hell with it, plenty of time to worry. It would be a long trip, and unless we caught a steady breeze going in pretty much the precise direction we needed to move, it would be a slow trip.

I gazed around at the flat sea. I sighed for the breeze, which was refreshing but useless. Squinted up at the sun and wondered if there was any way to build a sextant from available Everworld materials. Wondered if there was any point: After all,

for all we knew, Everworld was flat or concave or
shaped like a doughnut.

My gaze was drawn to a half-dozen flying fish
breaking the surface. And then I saw the sail off
the port bow. The distant sail bellied out with a
wind that did not exist.

Calm over. Storm about to begin.

Chapter
II

It was a smaller boat than ours, and faster. Maybe it was bringing up the wind, riding at the front of a new breeze, but I didn't believe it. Not from that direction, not running exactly counter to our own breeze. No. That boat was self-propelled somehow. There were no engines in Everworld — the place was not about technology — so whoever was in that boat was commanding the wind to rise just for him.

I looked at Senna. She was alert. Watching. Her gray eyes were dark with worry, the color of mercury.

"It's him," she said. "It's Merlin."

"Yeah. That was my guess, too."

We had evaded the old man in Egypt. He'd been called there by Senna's mother, but in the chaos of destruction that had followed we'd lost him.

As the strange boat closed in on us I could see the old man's long, once-blond, now grayish hair and beard, imagine his intelligent blue eyes, sunken beneath a lined brow. Remember what I'd seen him do — bring dead animals to life, make a wall rise from a pile of rubble, command a dragon to do his bidding, hold fierce Amazon warriors in suspension.

This was the wizard who wanted Senna, who wanted to keep her from Loki's clutches. Who would imprison her if he could, kill her if he had to.

Wasn't going to happen. Not if I could help it.

"Everyone up," I said. "We have trouble."

Jalil, Christopher, and April stirred, awoke with varying degrees of grace. Christopher shaded his eyes and stared. "It's freaking Merlin, man."

I called to Nikos. The captain was sitting in the shade under an awning, drinking wine with what had to be the first officer, a guy who occasionally stirred himself to yell at the rowers. The two of them were moderately drunk, but the sight of that sail sobered them pretty quickly.

"Captain? Can we outrun him?" Knew that it was a ridiculous question. How would the captain know the extent of Merlin's magic?

Nikos knew as well as I did that the other boat was not obeying the usual laws of sailing. "The gods will decide," he said with a fatalistic shrug.

"Well, kick the rowers into high gear," I said. "And raise sail. We may get close enough to ram him."

"This is my ship, friend," Nikos said. "I will decide. And I do not wish to offend the gods. No. That boat is too small to be a pirate; he cannot attempt to board and take us. I think he is interested in something else." He gave me a fish-eyed look that made it clear he was not risking his ship for our sakes. The gods wanted us badly enough to blow this boat toward us? Fine with him; he'd been paid, and the gods were welcome to us.

No point in threatening a fight: The crew was small for a ship this size, but Nikos still had sixty guys.

"You worry about the gods? This isn't about the gods. See her?" I pointed at Senna. "She's a witch. Raise sail or she turns your cargo into so much worm food."

The captain thought that over for a moment. There's a real shortage of skepticism in Everworld, and he never doubted my word that Senna was a witch. "Raise the sail," Nikos ordered. "We will run before the wind, but we will not outrun the will of the gods."

That was the extent of my brilliant plan. Raise sail and hope our fitful breeze would carry us away from Merlin's purposeful wind.

The rowers advanced their rhythm, the sail dropped, and we turned to take the wind from straight aft. The ship responded. I could feel it surge forward and I could see that it didn't make a damned bit of difference. The other boat would catch us. And then what? Was it Merlin alone? If so, maybe we could still keep him from boarding.

Then again, maybe not.

Didn't want to ask the others for ideas, though if someone made a brilliant suggestion, I'd put the plan in motion. Better Jalil's plan, or Christopher's, than no plan at all. No plan was what I had.

Senna? No. She had powers, but she was like a really good high-school player trying to go one-on-one with Shaq. She was a long way from taking Merlin down. What were we going to —

The sea erupted! The stretch of sea separating the two converging boats simply erupted — a pillar of water billowed and rose up — impossible.

It looked like some sort of bizarre Hollywood special effect. The sea was opening up, rising up, forming a twisting pillar of boiling green water. It looked like . . .

"It's like the Ten freaking Commandments!" Christopher yelled.

Exactly. Like the movie when the Israelites cross the Red Sea. But now the water was taking shape. A huge figure was emerging from the swirling green whirlpool. It undulated wildly, but still a vague outline was discernible. A man, a human, at least a creature vaguely resembling a human. A god. Had to be.

Like a massive, shifting, crudely human-shaped jellyfish. Translucent, like a giant blob of hair gel on the palm of the water, piled upon the water, rising from it.

And inside the creature, part of the creature, swimming around in its belly and brain, there were what looked a hell of a lot like dolphins and sharks and rays and other sea creatures I couldn't quite make out. Clumps of seaweed, for all I knew. Maybe whales — it was big enough.

The crew moaning and praying and wailing, the name Poseidon on every tongue. April, making the sign of the cross. Jalil, openmouthed, still in some way, on some level outraged by the mere fact of magic, the Everworld reality of charms, spells, physical laws broken and mended and broken again. Christopher, trembling, mumbling something about Charlton Heston, Pharoah, and "Let my freaking people go."

Senna, standing alone, facing the monstrosity, a cold wind making her hair blow straight back. Calculating. Wondering whether this was Merlin's doing or whether the sailors were right and this was some far greater power.

And then, the watery thing spoke.

The voice, if that's what it was — hard to tell with my eardrums near to bursting and my eyes closing against the sound, my feet slipping out from under me, knees hitting the wooden deck. The voice spoke, shouted, roared like a too, too loud surround-sound system in a too, too small movie theater. The voice seemed to come from the entire body of living water, from no one place in particular, no lips moving or tongue wagging.

"Who dares to command the winds and waters of mighty Neptune? Who dares use magic to challenge my will?"

It took me a second to get it. Neptune wasn't pissed at us. He was after Merlin!

I saw Merlin doing a quick bow-and-scrape and looking more nervous than I'd have thought possible.

"This arrogance, this impudence will not go unpunished," Neptune roared.

Then . . . he, it, Neptune was gone.

The squall attacked with such sudden violence it was like the concussion of a bomb. Winds of terrifying, irresistible force. The squall hit the sail, laid us over on our side. I slid, fell, tumbled down a deck suddenly as pitched as an IHOP roof.

I hit the rail, slammed hard, arm numbed.

A wall of green water swept over the ship. Would we come up? Would the boat swim?

The wave swept past, carrying away the mast, the sail, oars, many of the rowers, and all the crates and crap that had been stowed carelessly around the deck. The ship began to right itself, but so slowly, so heavily. It wallowed like a barrel. I spit water, clawed my way back to the oar, had to be able to steer — if the next wave caught us broadside we were all done.

"Row!" I bellowed. "Row, dammit!" The only hope was to get the ship moving, get her bow into the waves.

No rowers. The crew that hadn't been washed overboard was in a state of weeping panic.

I saw a soaked, battered Jalil stagger to a surviving oar, but no way, not one guy, wasn't happening, and now the second wave, the mother of all waves, was bearing down.

The deck fell away sickeningly as we slid into

the trough. The wave towered above us, towered above where the mast would have been. It was a mountain of water. No hope.

A hammer blow that caught me, snatched me away from my precarious hold on the steering oar, and carried me away, once more to be stopped by the bulwark. I was half drowned, dazed, bruised.

Still she swam. But the quinquireme was low in the water. Gunwales barely clear.

The crew, what was left, clung helplessly to rails and the stump of the mast. So did my friends. Hopeless. Another wave coming. Relentless. If we stayed any longer we'd go down, sucked down with the ship.

"Off the bow!" I yelled in the weird calm between waves. "Grab an oar, jump! Go, go, go!"

I saw April running. Christopher limping. The deck tilted perilously. We were stern on to the wave. Now we were rolling, falling toward the bow. Christopher jumped. Where was Senna?

The wave . . . I jumped.

CHAPTER

III

The wave lifted the boat nearly vertical, slammed into the stern, and drove the ship down like a spike under a sledgehammer's blow. The ship speared into the water and then disappeared.

"Senna!"

Suction caught me, a swirling drain with me no more than a bug.

Blinded by salt water and confusion and pain, I put one hand over my head, palm flat up, and kicked, used my left arm as a paddle, had to get to the surface, hell, I could be on the surface, couldn't tell, woozy, head hurt.

Remember, David, save yourself first, be able to save the others. . . .

Palm hit something hard, better than hitting

with my head. I felt along the object, lungs beginning to burn, still blind, kicked to my left, used the free arm again to propel myself beyond the barrier, strong stroke down . . . broke free!

Air! I took deep, deep breaths, another slap of water almost choked me, rushed down into my lungs. I coughed, gagged, rubbed my eyes until they opened, blink, blink, had to find the others, had to find Senna!

I grabbed a floating timber. All that was left.

"Who's there?!" I shouted, but I didn't know if anyone could hear my voice over the boiling sea, a sea tormented into an artificial frenzy by Neptune, a sea meant to kill us. A sky lowering and black, a sky now raining hailstones like bullets.

Impossible to see. The waves were mountains around me. I rose with the swell, was swamped by the crest, then slid down the far side of the wave.

Then . . . through the needlelike spray and biting foam, a form, a figure. I kicked, thrust my arms through the water, breaststroked, dogpaddled, anything to fight my way through the chaotic sea, to get closer to that form, that person. . . .

"April! April, hold on!"

Struggling, flailing manically, long hair streaked across her face, wound around her neck like an oil slick. April. I swam, saw her gulp about a gallon of water. Saw her eyes close, saw her slip under, one pale hand.

No! One more awkward stroke, thrust, lunge, and I would be there. Where? Where had she gone down, exactly? I was exhausted, confused, in the middle of a wrathful storm, but no choice, I had to try. Gulping air, as much as I could hold through the sudden overwhelming weariness, I dove, tried to open my eyes, managed a slit, felt stupidly around with my hands, crying silently, *April, April, April.*

Had to come up for air. *No use to anyone dead, right, David?* Gasping, pulling wet, heavy hair off my forehead, yanking my eyes open with my hands. Nothing, no one, only debris in this watery canyon.

I took another deep breath and, shivering, teeth chattering, prepared to dive again, and again, as many times as it took, when I was hit from behind. A jagged piece of the destroyed ship, I couldn't guess more than that, speared me in the back and thrust me under the angry waters. The fear–sickness overtook me. I couldn't breathe, couldn't think straight, I was disoriented — had I reached the surface again? Couldn't tell, because now my body was being turned round and round, I was revolving, twirling, like some half-smoked cigarette tossed in a flushing toilet.

Panic and struggling and inhaling water and more panic, more struggling, now vertigo, nausea. I knew about sailing, I knew about drowning, knew the causes and stages and how to try to revive a near-drowning victim. I knew all this and forgot every bit of it as I began to drown in that violently whirling sea. Neck snapping with each revolution around and down and around and down Neptune's whirlpool, the final force sent to finish us off. Spine cracking, arms and legs slapped to my side then torn away, flung wide, somehow I knew this but could not really feel my body, arms, legs. Could not see — were my eyes open or shut? Could not hear — was I imagining the roar of water, hallucinating the scream of wind? Could not breathe, could not think, could not live . . .

All over. All over. I sucked in water, but it didn't matter, nothing mattered because it was over.

And I breathed. Gagged, wretched, but breathed

and did not die. Choked but breathed again and habit or instinct made me spit it out, the water that I was breathing but still, I breathed and was alive.

How how how how? And I was sinking, slowly, gently, down down down, my eyes open, unstung by salt, open and aware and what, what was that I was seeing beneath me, what was I falling toward? Maybe I was dead after all, unconscious at least, imagining, dreaming, hallucinating, and this was my dream of heaven or whatever world there was beyond death. Funny, I'd never thought I had the creative power to come up with something so . . .

No, not a dream, no hallucination, somehow I knew that. Something told me I was there, taking up physical space, alive, observing the scene I was about to become a part of.

And not only me because now I could see Jalil close by, others, some of the sailors, and yes, April, now Senna, Christopher, all of us slowly floating downward, alive, unbelievably alive. Senna caught my eye, moved her lips but I couldn't hear or guess at what she was saying. After a moment she looked away.

Below us was a city. I might have been skydiving, falling toward it. A city. With tiled roofs and neatly laid-out streets. Roofs? Why, to keep out the rain? People down there. Swimming? Walking? It was crazy. I was wrong, I was hallucinating. Had to be. So far down below the surface of the water, how was it possible to see so clearly? Why wasn't everything shrouded in complete blackness; where was the light source; what was the light source?

Why was I bothering to wonder? W.T.E.

CHAPTER
IV

It was a city or town, surrounded by a sort of mountain range of coral, or something a lot like coral, rounded peaks in white, natural caves creating areas of dark, undulating sections in a pinkish-orange. Dotting or decorating the coral range, along its entire circumference I guessed, though from my ever-descending vantage point I couldn't see the far side of the range, were shoots and clumps of seaweed and other aquatic plants in different shapes, some short and plump, others tall and weedy, and in the entire range of colors from pea green to acid blue, from pale yellow to white spotted with red.

Nibbling at the vegetation, slipping into and out of the caves, were fish of all sorts. Long and skinny; short, flat, and wide; muddy coloring and pebbly skin; sleek bodies in shimmering purple.

Inside that coral bowl were structures, buildings and what seemed to be free-standing monuments, some built in the coral or coral-like material, some mimicking the coral's natural, asymmetrical formations, some looking an awful lot like — yeah, like stuff right out of ancient Rome. Like the things we'd seen at Olympus. A huge triumphal arch. An arena that might have been a Disney version of the Colosseum.

I flashed on something Athena had said, about Poseidon being on the outs with his brother Zeus, wondered if that meant Poseidon's Roman counterpart — Neptune — was also feuding with Zeus, maybe also with Poseidon. But the thought was gone as soon as I realized I could see individual people moving along streets, could see chariots whipping by, vehicles pulled by oversized sea horses and dolphins — as soon as I realized that a huge bubble encased the city and in less than two minutes I was going to break right through it. Weird. The bubble enclosed air, but it enclosed water, too. The city had areas of normal atmosphere, areas where the streets surged with water. The bubble had bubbles within.

Ride the big bubble, David. I concentrated on flipping my body facedown, not hard to do, then on spreading my arms and legs wide to distribute my weight, to make me, hopefully, less of a projectile or bullet, maybe something that might rest on top of the bubble, not piercing it, maybe not destroying the city and seriously pissing off its resident, presiding god. Though what I would do next if I didn't fall through to the underwater city, remained balanced on the bubble, I didn't really think about.

Closer, closer still. I didn't dare risk looking around again for the others. Hoped they were watching me, trying to do what I was doing. Or maybe they had better ideas.

I kept my eyes on the city, noticed now I was heading right for the arena. Noticed that on the floor of the arena there was a racetrack of some sort. Reviewing stands, cheering crowds, I was falling right on top of all that. I pretended, told myself I was as light as a feather, weightless, that bodies in water had buoyancy, what was I worried about, I'd land gently on the city's bubble roof and then . . .

And then I felt the skin of the bubble meet my flesh and a sensation I'd never experienced. I became one with the skin. It stretched across my limbs, torso, molded itself against my face like stretched elastic wrap, but soft, gentle, then seemed to pass behind me, to leave my skin with a tickle, caress my head and the back of my neck and pass beyond. But the skin had not moved, had not gone anywhere. I was the one moving, I was still falling, floating sweetly down, closer to the residents of this place. I lifted my head to see the large bubble unbroken above me. And closer to my head . . . I reached out my hand and felt another skin. Now I was in my own bubble, protective or restraining, a womb or a prison, it didn't matter, what the hell was happening . . .

Closer to the ground, right over a far corner of the arena, off to the side of what was definitely a roughly oval racetrack, not far from what I took to be the finishing line where the race was ending in a rush and roar. I had the absurd feeling that I was floating down into Wrigley Field but that none of the fans cared enough to notice.

Closer . . . My feet hit the ground, then my knees, and the small bubble burst, depositing me on the hard-packed sand.

Muffled thumps behind me. I turned. Christopher, then the Greek captain. Then, more sailors, but by no means most of them, then Jalil, Senna, April, bubbles popping, dropping their contents to the ground.

No Merlin.

"Where are we?" April asked, the first to get her head straight.

Her words were swallowed up in an anticipatory roar from the crowd. The horses for the next race were coming onto the track. It was a roar that warbled weirdly: The stands were underwater. The roar of the crowd sounded like people yelling from the bottom of a swimming pool.

Obviously we were not anyone's top priority right then. We were off the track, a small, forlorn knot of people, irrelevant to the racing fans.

"Ben Hur," Christopher muttered. "Ben Hur meets the Little freaking Mermaid, man."

The captain stated the obvious. "We are in Neptune's realm," he wailed. "If only it was Poseidon."

"Is there a difference?" Jalil muttered, looking even skinnier soaking wet.

"Both are terrible in their anger," the captain answered.

"One prefers pasta, the other likes gyros. Jesus, look at this place." Christopher, of course. He babbles when he's scared.

I dropped my hand to my sword hilt and squeezed the hard, reassuring steel. That's what I do when I'm scared.

We were in air. Standing on dry land. The track itself was a pocket of air, but the reviewing stands were behind a curved, arched wall of water. It was like looking into an aquarium. From an air bubble inside the aquarium. The entire mass of magically restrained water looked as if it might crash down on us at any moment. I had the sense of being a bug about to be crushed by a sledgehammer.

"We've done gods," April said. "How much worse could Neptune be?"

"You cannot compare the glorious gods of the Greeks to their pale Roman imitators!" the captain stated hotly. His crew, which had moved close, now edged away nervously. No one was anxious to cast aspersions on Neptune.

"Our gods, from great Father Zeus to the most lowly messenger gods, are gracious models of gentle humanity compared to the craven, spineless gods of the debauched Roman people."

He sounded shrill and he glanced over his shoulder as he said all this. And he'd noticed that suddenly no one was standing within thunderbolt range of him. I turned to Senna. She looked as shaken up as the rest of us, but stood, as was her habit, a bit apart.

"Do you know anything about Neptune?" I asked quietly.

She laughed. "Here's what I know: We're miles under the surface of the ocean, in the power of a Roman god. And Merlin managed to follow us out of Egypt. And as much as I'd like to think the old man's drowned, I'm not counting on it. We, on the other hand, could be drowned very suddenly, very finally."

"Could be, but we're not, which by rights we should be," April pointed out, finding the one small ray of optimism.

"Yeah? Well, stick around. The day is young," Senna said.

As if to underline her statement, a dozen trumpets all blared out, announcing that the next race was about to begin.

CHAPTER
V

There was a clap of thunder and the horses were off. They came pounding around the bend of the oval track.

The horses were large, larger than the largest real-world horses I'd ever seen, large in the way so many things were large in Everworld: in impossible proportions, proportions that had nothing to do with real-world physics. The horses were white, blazingly bright, built like thoroughbreds, with sleek, trim bodies, long legs, long narrow necks. But unlike real-world thoroughbreds, and so appropriate for Everworld, these horses had long, flowing manes of what had to be spun gold. And their hooves — definitely bronze, and gleaming.

"I don't know why I keep saying this," Jalil

muttered under his breath, "but none of this is possible."

Riding the horses were elves, looking smaller than ever on the backs of the huge horses. The elves didn't so much straddle the horses' backs as perch there on top, crouched down in typical jockey position.

And in the reviewing stands or bleachers, whatever they were called in ancient Rome, watching the race, cheering, talking, laughing, the usual once-mind-blowing, now-to-be-expected variety of beings. A cornucopia of species and nationalities. All sitting, standing, milling around behind their shimmering wall of water.

There were humans: white, black, Asian, and undetermined. All breathing water. Breathing. Talking. Laughing. Drinking. Underwater.

There were nymphs in their usual array of colors, translucent and opaque, green, blue, and yellow, seated next to leering brown and black satyrs, who, given their particular bodies, stood. And leered.

There were elves, delicate and beautiful, Lara Flynn Boyle thin, male and female equally ethereal. They looked strangely at home in the water.

There were dwarves, taciturn, tough-looking, short but as broad as they were tall. Bristling

beards, always an ax or some other sort of
weapon or tool at their sides. You could sense
something dangerous about dwarves, something
not evil but serious and purposeful and not ever
in the mood for nonsense. Their hair and beards
floated weirdly around their faces.

There were trolls, too, which I was not happy
to see. They're stupid, rocklike things, servants
and soldiers of Loki. Maybe other gods as well.
Who knows, maybe there's a special troll employ-
ment agency.

From the back, trolls looked headless. From the
front, you saw a sort of slung-forward rhinolike
head with a long, blunt snout and blank little
piglike eyes. Either view was unfortunate. The
water gave them a faintly blue cast. And there
were representatives of the two alien species we'd
encountered in Everworld: the Coo-Hatch and
the Hetwan. God knows what the Coo-Hatch
were doing there: It was hard to imagine the ob-
sessive metallurgists being happy in a place
where no forge could be lit.

But the elves, dwarves, fairies, nymphs, satyrs,
Coo-Hatch, and Hetwan were old news. There
were other species here as well, scatterings of
shapes and faces and skin colors we had not yet
encountered.

Then there were the locals.

"Mermaids," Christopher said, nodding and suppressing a grin.

"Mermen, too," April agreed.

"Really? I hadn't noticed them," Christopher said dryly. "Noticed the mermaids, though. Noticed the hell out of the mermaids."

From the waist down they were sleek, muscular fish covered in gleaming scales of pale blue and cotton-candy pink and sparkling silver, ending in translucent, fanlike tails.

From the waist up they were male or female — human male or female. The men were a powerful-looking crew, rippling biceps and rock-hard pecs. And they seemed particularly numerous right around the fifty-yard line where Neptune himself and a crowd of minor gods, hangers-on, and toadies lounged comfortably. My guess was that the mermen were Neptune's honor guard.

The female mermaids, on the other hand, were not at all threatening. They had slender arms, straight shoulders, long, flowing hair, magazine-ad hair, TV-spokesmodel hair, deep red and bright gold and lustrous black. Hair which, when the water wafted it just the right way, discreetly covered them.

But, to the frank delight of Christopher in particular, the water seldom placed the hair with perfect discretion. "I'll tell you right now, David, if they have beer in this place, I'm staying. Forever."

April opened her mouth to say something crushing, but whatever she was about to say was cut off by a mammoth cheer that rose warbling and gurgly from the stands. Voices were accompanied by the trumpetlike sound of conch shells blown like horns.

The race was coming down the stretch with two horses neck and neck ahead of the pack. The crowd was on its feet and tails, urging and yelling and applying body English, just like any bunch of normal race fans.

Neptune stood now, too, an imposing presence at well over ten feet tall. His court all stood and the nearest mermen bristled and surveyed the crowd, looking for trouble like a bunch of Secret Service agents.

The race ended. The final horse crossed the finish line. And all at once Neptune was somehow on this side of the water wall, on the floor of the arena, in the winner's circle.

With him had come several mermen, definitely bodyguards, looking tough even while balancing — how? — on their relatively flimsy fish tails. There were also a few people dressed in togas who I thought might be minor gods, or maybe just rich guys.

After another moment, Neptune signaled for silence. Immediately, the crowd grew still. Instantly. As if an extra millisecond of unsanctioned rowdiness might be a death-penalty offense.

The god began to speak in a voice much less outrageously loud than the one he'd used on the surface. Tolerable, but not exactly enjoyable.

"I am Neptune, the great Earth-Shaker, the Flooder, father of the mighty Cyclops, progenitor of the glorious Theseus, sire of the giant twins Otus and Ephialtes. It is to me that conch-blowing, sea-calming Triton, king of the mer-people, owes his life. To me Delphinus attributes his starry presence in the heavens. To me Neleus and Pelias are ever thankful.

"I am Neptune! Manly husband to Amphitrite, the beautiful sister to lovely Thetis. I am Neptune! Forceful lover of Medusa, so cruelly changed by jealous Athena into a snake-haired gorgon. Would-be lover of Scylla, so meanly transformed by jealous Amphitrite into a many-headed monster." He shot a dirty look at a beautiful goddess who I assumed must be Amphitrite. Then he smiled a benevolent, indulgent smile. "Of course, I have forgiven Amphitrite.

"I am Neptune!" he resumed. "Parent with mighty Earth of invincible Antaeus. Father, too, to hundred-handed Briareus . . ."

"Boy gets around, doesn't he?" Christopher whispered.

"Don't they all?" Jalil muttered.

"And I have been pleased and entertained by this race of magnificent beasts. I accord the laurel wreath to Tyro, a worthy animal named after the mother of my sons Neleus and Pelias, and to her elfin rider, former resident of Dragonwood, now devoted to serving the renowned stables of Neptune, founder and inventor of the magnificent sport of horse racing."

The crowd, which had to have heard this self-serving oration before, sat and floated rapt, attentive, hanging on every word under the intimidating scowl of the mermen. They interrupted to applaud at several points, crying out praises and compliments.

It was quite a performance. It married the ludicrous, over-the-top enthusiasm of an infomercial to the posturing and toadying of a Nazi rally.

Still we stood there, ignored by Neptune and his people, a loose group of real-worlders and cowering Greek sailors. Watched as Neptune congratulated the winner of the race, grabbed the horses's snout and kissed her soundly, bowed graciously to the rider, an elf in a pink silk shirt and pants curiously similar to contemporary real-world racing silks.

We stood and watched and waited and I wondered where Merlin had gone. Had he been killed or injured in the storm? Was he vulnerable to Neptune's powers, or had he been miraculously preserved, as we had? I scanned the crowd. Was he standing among the throngs right now, disguised as something other than an old wizard? Was he hiding?

Finally, Neptune completed his adoration of the horse and rider — mostly of the horse — and turned in our direction. He seemed to notice us for the first time, bedraggled, soaked, the survivors of his freak storm.

"I am so not liking the look in this guy's eye," Christopher mumbled.

Neptune spoke. His voice was bored. "Greek sailors, yes? Pigs. Away, away, away with them," he said, flipping his hand at his wrist and making a pout. "Wait!" His eyes narrowed, the expression of a foppish dilettante instantly replaced by a suspicious frown. "Where is the troublemaker? The one who was alone in his boat, the one meddling with my affairs? A wizard if I do not miss my guess."

There was a low murmuring among those servants and bodyguards and hangers-on closest to

Neptune, heads swiveled to scan the arena, shoulders shrugged. No one came right out and said, "I don't know, Neptune, sir. He's gone. You can kill me now and boil my liver for dinner."

But it didn't seem to matter. In another instant, the god sighed and replaced his frown with a look of disinterest. "No matter," he said, with another flip of his wrist. "Kill these who remain."

No sooner said than done because at that moment, even before Neptune's final word had died on my ears, half a dozen sharks appeared. They swam down just inches above the heads of the spectators, eliciting appreciative oohs and ahs and anticipatory giggles.

The sharks were not large by Everworld standards, but plenty large. None was less than twenty feet long. Twenty feet long and hungry. With a sudden, spasmodic downward jerk, one of the sharks snatched a dwarf from his seat and bit him in two.

The legs, still kicking, floated down trailing a cloud of blood. The crowd shrieked. Those nearest panicked but those sitting farther away loved it. Neptune laughed his mad laugh, and the laugh was echoed from every wet corner of the colosseum.

Neptune and his boys were just as suddenly back on the other side of the wall, back in their comfortable seats, settling in for the spectacle of slaughter.

"They can't get out, can they?" Christopher wailed.

"Great Athena save us!" Nikos cried.

The nearest shark swam right up to the barrier separating water and air. Then it kept swimming. As its snout emerged, a water bubble formed, encasing the beast.

The shark, within its undulating bubble, swam floating through the air. Mouth open now. Rows and rows of serrated triangular teeth.

Straight for us.

VI

Another shark in its bubble, and another, and another. Six in all. They slid through the water wall and undulated swiftly toward us.

"Scatter, break up," I shouted. "Maybe we can make them chase us, tire them out, maybe they won't get us all. Now!"

I dove to the left, threw myself aside just as one of the sharks torpedoed straight for me. I rolled, drew my sword, stabbed straight upward as the shark skimmed overhead. Hit nothing but water.

"Aaah!"

I spun, just in time to see one of the sailors drawn inside one of the water bubbles. It was over quickly then, sharp, slanted teeth tearing at soft human flesh, chomping on bloody intestines, the interior of the bubble becoming opaque with a red cloud of blood and guts.

Then, another screaming, writhing sailor snatched, this time dragged one arm, one leg in the bubble, the other arm and leg out of the bubble, through the wall of water and torn apart, ingested to the roaring, waterlogged approval of the crowd.

I ran, sword drawn. Too slow. The shark was doing a sort of victory lap, dragging what was now a corpse. Blood and water ran down the body, trailing red in the dirt.

Another marauding shark, and another sailor crunched like a cookie before I could lunge, thrust. I was a fool, running, racing, stabbing at animals who were far faster than I and outnumbered me six to one. Hard choices: Protect my own.

I ran toward where April and Christopher huddled close together. Jalil was not far off with his tiny Coo-Hatch pocketknife open.

But then it dawned on me. The sharks were not coming after us, me, Jalil, Christopher, April, Senna. The sharks had herded the remaining sailors into a tight huddle from which, one by one, a sailor was cut and run down.

No, not all the remaining sailors, David, not all, one is apart, one seems to be unnoticed, off on his own, didn't really remember his face from the boat but . . .

Fine. The sharks weren't bothering us, that didn't mean I was going to stand by doing nothing. I stumbled forward, ran toward one of the circling sharks. Gripped the hilt of my sword with both hands, closer, closer, raised the sword high, raised the sword of Galahad and with a grunt I struck down with all my strength.

The sword cut water, cut scale and flesh and cartilage. I cut the shark in two just ahead of its tail. The sword had slid right through the bubble casing to split the animal and now slipped back out. And in the still-floating, undamaged bubble, two pieces of a shark hung suspended, blood coloring the water.

For a moment, there was relative silence as the crowd no doubt processed the fact that a human condemned to death by Neptune had just killed one of the god's executioners. I glanced at the others. Their faces showed fear, satisfaction, and traces of anger on Senna's. Too bad. I'd had to do it, couldn't just sit around and wait for more people to be murdered, wait to be killed myself by the arbitrary orders of yet another sicko god.

Neptune raised his hand and the attacks ceased. The sharks swam agitated circles within their globes.

"Who are you, mortal?" Neptune demanded.

"Who are you to come uninvited to my domain and then so boldly kill my shark? Such a display of bravery amuses me. Speak!"

In his face, no other way. If I wimped he'd kill me; I was completely certain of that. I sheathed my sword, rested my hand on the hilt. Back straight, eyes raised to the Roman god, I stepped forward.

"I am the commander of the Greek armies defending Olympus against the Hetwan armies of Ka Anor," I said loudly, arrogantly. "Wise Athena calls me General Davideus and I am sworn to defend and protect what is hers."

Jalil stepped up behind me, giving support, backing my play. And giving me grief at the same time. "You do know this is a Roman god, right?" he said in a voiceless whisper. "And his Greek counterpart supposedly has a particular hard-on for Athena."

"He hates Athena? That would have been useful information. About ten seconds ago," I muttered.

Neptune raised his trident, his telephone-pole-sized trident with three barbed spear points. His massive, unbearded face was a mask of fury, veins bulging and pumping in his forehead, along his neck.

"No!" April, shouting, waving her hands, smiling her big, Hollywood smile. "A joke! Mighty Neptune, great Neptune, he jests!" Manically, she pointed back at me. "He, David, this one, he is our fool! We are minstrels, minstrels from the old world with wonderful tales and lively songs never before heard in Everworld. And we would be honored, honored, great, er, sir, if you would allow us to perform for your pleasure."

There was a horrible moment of waiting, waiting for the god to buy our story, the story we'd been telling since the Viking days, the story explaining our presence in Everworld, a story everyone had believed. So far.

The hand that grasped the trident was still poised above the god's curly head. An insane anger, or maybe just insanity, blazed from his dark eyes, what I could see of them from under his bunched brow.

And then . . .

Neptune shrugged. Lowered the trident. A grin every bit as false as April's spread over his face. "Very well. You minstrels, you may have the honor of entertaining me. But not now, later, soon, when I am better in the mood." Neptune sighed, a gale of wind. "I am a weary god," he admitted, pouting. "War is brewing in my underwater kingdom, war between myself and that interloper Poseidon, that Greek bastard, that thief! I was the first to carry the trident with which to command the waves and rake the sea! I, great Neptune, not womanish Poseidon! I defy anyone to refute my claim, which is just and right. I defy anyone to stand in my way as I claim Atlantis as my own! You! Do you defy me?"

I turned to look at the person Neptune had singled out to be the recipient of his wrath. A human, a man, dark-haired, copper-skinned, sitting in the stands. An Aztec perhaps, looking alarmed, eyes widened, mouth open.

He stood slowly. "No . . . no, Great Neptune . . ."

Neptune grinned and wiggled his eyebrows. "Oh, I think you do!" he sang. And threw the trident at the man. The middle of the three prongs pierced the man's heart. The other two prongs buried themselves deep in the rock of the stands. The man was killed instantly.

"Oh, God," April whispered.

Neptune was no longer calm. He had been calm for about five seconds, and then had revved up to insanity and arbitrarily killed an innocent bystander, and now he was pissed and pitiful.

"My trident, my lovely trident! Spoiled by the foul blood of a traitor! Oh, oh, bring me a new trident, burn the other, hurry, hurry. . . ."

"This guy's nuts," Christopher whispered. "Not just the usual nutty god — I mean he's a total whack job."

We stood there, watching a nymph servant smooth Neptune's brow, another bring him something in a goblet, two more rush off, presumably to snag a spare trident.

But we hadn't been forgotten. Two mermen appeared before us. I hadn't even seen them coming. These guys could swim. And, it seemed, they could move through the air as easily as if through water.

"You will come away now," the larger of the two said. "You will rest until great Neptune commands your presence."

Jalil shot me a look. I nodded. Not much else to do but follow these guys. At least get out of Neptune's immediate range. Then, assess the situation, make a plan. Stay alive.

I breathed. First time in a while. But I didn't relax. I could feel that trident emerging from the wall of water, whistling through the air, piercing me through, severing my spine, nailing me to the . . .

Okay, keep it together, David. Just walk out of the damned place with your head up and you can have a breakdown later.

We followed the two mermen from the arena

and I noticed the sailor, the one who hadn't been rounded up with the others, one of the few surviving sailors. He was walking, unmolested — why wasn't anyone stopping him? — walking away at a right angle to us. I thought I should call to him, ask him to join us, but didn't.

I had a pretty good idea of why this particular sailor should be able to walk away unnoticed.

VII

We followed the mermen who, unaccountably, swam through the air without benefit of water.

We followed them out of the colosseum by way of a tunnel that dead-ended in a wall of water. The mermen simply swam from air to water with barely a pause or a ripple.

We stopped. One of the mermen looked back, scowled, and motioned us forward.

"Dude. We kind of need air," Christopher said.

I could see a city ahead. Streets. Buildings. Sidewalk vendors. Beasts of burden. I saw humans ahead, humans walking and talking and presumably breathing underwater. Logic told me the mermen were not out to drown us. Logic told me it was okay, that if Neptune wanted us dead he'd find a more dramatic way. To hell with logic. That was a wall of water. Real water. The kind you can't breathe without gills.

Jalil stepped forward, lips pursed like maybe he was going to start whistling. He stepped up and reached out a tentative hand to touch the wall of water. He drew his hand back and looked at the wetness.

"What, you thought maybe it was fake water?" Christopher asked.

Jalil looked a little embarrassed, an emotion he conveys by pressing his lips into a line and narrowing his eyes angrily. He stuck his hand into the water and moved it around. Then he sucked in a deep breath and poked his whole head into the water.

And yet, he did not breathe. Not till the veins were popping out of his neck and his chest was heaving. Then, all at once, he inhaled.

His eyes flew open. He breathed again.

Then with an effort of will he stepped fully through the water barrier and stood there calmly breathing, in and out, in and out. No bubbles. Just one of the weirdnesses. No bubbles.

"I never knew Jalil could show such faith in the power of magic," Senna mocked.

"The power of reason," Jalil countered, his

voice warbly and indistinct. "What is, is. There are people in here breathing."

Senna laughed, dismissing that as so much nonsense. And she stepped through. The water lifted her hair and swirled it into a golden cloud. She laughed again, sheer delight this time. Senna liked magic, the fact of it, the power of it, in a way none of us shared.

April was next. Then Christopher.

I was not being the fearless leader. I have a thing about smothering. I'm against it. There were a lot of ways to die and having my lungs fill with water was not my favorite.

"Come on in, Aquaman," Christopher said.

"Screw you."

I wasn't going to panic. Couldn't. But I'd come pretty near to drowning once already, and with that memory fresh in my mind I wasn't anxious to try it again. April stepped back through, wet, bedraggled. She started to take my hand and guide me in.

No. That wasn't happening. Not with the mermen smirking at me.

I didn't exactly slap her hand away, but I did push past her and run straight into the wall of water. Closed my eyes, an instinct, held my breath.

Then, I breathed. My lungs filled with water. I

could feel it. It was cold, colder than air. A heaviness. I wanted to gag, which was my first instinct, but I resisted.

Exhale. Exhale thick, viscous water.

I moved and I moved like a guy underwater. God help me if I tried to use my sword. But I could see. And when I tried to talk, my voice sounded almost normal in my ears. My clothes billowed around me.

"Well, this is definitely different," I said.

"First time we've all been clean at the same time since Olympus," April noted.

I gave a nod to the mermen. "Lead on."

The mermen were powerful creatures in the air. But now, in their natural element, their superiority was even more obvious. They moved with the ease of dolphins. Slight kicks of their powerful tails were all it took for them to outpace our labored, bobbling, men-on-the-moon steps.

For the first time I noticed the foot-long coral blades at the mermen's sides. If it came to a fight between me and them it was going to be short and unpleasant.

"David Boreanaz," April said.

"David what?"

"Angel. You know, from *Buffy*? He's got his own show now, bad vampire turned good vampire. This merman looks like him. From the waist up, I mean."

"I don't watch much TV. I watch the Bulls and the Bears and Northwestern whenever they have a game on TV."

"David's too mature to watch TV," Christopher said.

"I'm sorry I'm not up on all of April's latest teen crushes," I snapped.

April laughed. "David's a little tense."

"Yeah. I wonder why," I muttered.

"So, April, what you're saying is that you like a guy with no hair on his chest? Kind of that girlie-man look?" Christopher went on. "You don't go for someone more, I don't know, virile, manly? Someone like our general here?"

"No, I like a man with a definite feminine side, Christopher. So there's hope for you."

Christopher brayed a watery laugh.

I was glad they could joke around. Really was. But I wasn't feeling relaxed myself. How exactly were we supposed to escape from this place? I had no illusions: Our ability to breathe underwater was magic, Neptune's magic. Magic that could be withdrawn at any moment.

The merman led us to what might have been a typical house of ancient Rome or Pompeii or whatever. I wouldn't know. The two of them stood — or floated — by the door and motioned for us to go on in. They took up positions as guards, already looking bored.

Inside the house we found a small, open center courtyard surrounded on all four sides by columns that helped support a series of small rooms. To go from one room to the next you had to cross the courtyard or move around the inner perimeter. An inconvenience if it rained. Not a problem here.

The walls were painted with pictures of birds and flowers, fish and coral reefs, surprisingly realistic landscapes and seascapes. Also, pictures of men and women and mermen and mermaids, average people by Neptune's standards.

In at least one, no, two of these pictures, the mermen and maids were engaged in blatantly erotic activities. The pictures were framed by borders, a sort of interlocking key pattern, and by painted architectural features, like columns, windows opening onto vistas, and moldings.

One wall panel, though, painted like the others with a deep, strong red, black, a kind of dark yellow, showed what April figured was some kind of ceremony or triumphal procession starring Neptune and his wife. The two gods, wearing what looked a lot like halos around their heads, both naked to the waist, were standing in a chariot drawn through the sea by four large horses.

Around them cavorted various types of flat fish, octopuses, and less usual specimens that looked like small aquatic dragons. Flying above Neptune and Amphitrite were two fat little angels with tiny wings holding either end of a billowing piece of fabric so that it formed an arch over the heads of the gods.

The floors were done in mosaics, small pieces of colored tile arranged to depict everything from bunches of grapes to barking dogs to some conch-blowing god who seemed, from the context, to be Neptune's son.

What was amazing was the fact that Neptune and Amphitrite and Triton were not idealized images drawn from imagination. They were portraits of the real individuals.

Other than the rich decoration of walls and floors, with themes from above and below the surface of the sea, the house was empty of all but the essential furnishings, like a few short, narrow beds in a few of the rooms around the courtyard, simple chairs, and a table.

"A typical ancient Roman dwelling, I'd imagine," Jalil said. "Except for the fact that it's underwater. Someone want to explain how you paint underwater? Why are the roofs slanted? So the rain will run off? For that matter, why is it light? Does anyone see a sun? And why do I keep asking these questions?"

"Because you like to remind us how smart you are?" Christopher asked with false innocence.

"Oh, yeah, that's right. That's why," Jalil said.

"I'm liking our place on Olympus better," Christopher said. "The staff was a lot more friendly, great room service, and the humidity way less of a problem."

Underwater. No way to get used to that.

Breathing water, living in water made me feel powerless, unanchored, sapped of strength, not able to feel my proper weight or place in space. Like when you're in a swimming pool, and you feel suspended, light, like you weigh almost nothing, although that experience can be pleasant, because you're not battling lunatic despot gods.

This feeling was more like when every underwater motion you make is frustratingly slow and somehow delayed. When watching your own fingers try to pick up a quarter from the bottom of the deep end of the pool you feel a bit like a baby who hasn't gotten down his coordination, who can't quite direct his thumb and forefinger to pick the Cheerio up off the highchair tray on the first try. That experience is never pleasant.

"Guard!" I yelled.

One of the merman swam in, eyes flashing, angry at being summoned. Fine. Nice to know he wasn't impervious.

I said, "We're not fish. Do you think it's possible for us to stay someplace where we can breathe air?"

"Yeah," Christopher said. "Us being surface-dwellers and all. Lungs, no gills."

The merman's anger was replaced by insolence and contempt. He didn't deign to answer. With a flamboyant flip of his golden tail, he left, the door closing behind him.

But suddenly . . . air! Like the merman had thrown a switch. April's red hair, Senna's blond hair ceased to float around their heads and stream behind them, and fell to their shoulders. Earth-girl hair once again. My shirt, what remained of it, no longer billowed, now lay flat against my chest and stomach. I saw this all more clearly now, vividly, not through a piece of film that rendered everything slightly hazy, softened at the edges, colors dimmed.

Gravity. I felt the heaviness of my body, solid thigh muscles, feet firmly planted on the ground, skin dry and chapped from elements other than water, from cold air and biting wind and rough rock. This was better. I put my hand on the hilt of my sword. Could actually feel the metal, the rotted leather. Touch had returned, the full spectrum of touch and tangibility.

Jalil shook his head. "Impossible." He walked to a window, pulled open the shutters. "Unbelievable."

All around the house, pressing up against the air that filled the house to the invisible physical place where the inside of the house met the outside — water. Not rushing in to swamp the house, just there, seeming to press, threatening to embrace, to overwhelm. Jalil placed his hand against the wall of water, let it slip into the water. It looked like his hand had slipped inside the skin of a giant soap bubble, the kind that kids make by dipping a perforated plastic pan in soapy water and waving it through the air. But the bubble didn't break, still no leak or flood. He withdrew his hand, shook it dry.

"Okay, that's not too weird. My hand passed right through. There's not even a sheath or some other sort of barrier between the air and water. Nothing's holding them apart. That I can see, anyway. Equal and opposite forces . . ."

"Of course something's holding them apart."
Senna. She stood leaning against the far wall,
arms folded. "Neptune is holding his natural atmosphere and ours apart. Neptune is letting us
breath in water. Neptune is filling this house with
air. Magic, Jalil, deal with it. Neptune is granting
us life. He decides to withdraw his support, we're
dead. Your instinctive defiance isn't really very
helpful now."

Senna laughed and moved away from the wall.
"You are all so naive, so stubborn. And so blind.
Don't you see the beauty of it all? Are you all
completely unmoved by this?"

"The fishies are very nice," Christopher said.

April was wringing the water from her hair.
"That's not what she means. It's the power that's
beautiful to Senna. She's looking at all of this and
imagining having this power herself."

Senna didn't deny it. April was right, of course.

"Look," I said, "we might as well try to catch
some sleep. If anyone can sleep. We'll try to hook
up on the other side. Try to . . . I don't know." I
was suddenly just exhausted. "I've got first watch.
We're the minstrels, right? Guess we'd better be
ready to put on a show."

Jalil touched one of the beds. Felt the thin
blanket. "It's dry."

I let them go to sleep. I stepped out into the

courtyard and looked up. The wall of water hung above me. A mile or more of water.

How do you win a fight when your opponent has only to withdraw the magic that keeps you alive?

CHAPTER
VIII

"Oh, son of — !"

I turned the wheel sharply to the right, brought the Buick Beast back into the lane, winced as the guy coming the other way, the guy in the ten-year-old gray Mazda I'd almost hit head on, leaned on his horn, gave me the finger as he passed.

Okay, I deserved that. CNN: Breaking News. I was in my car, driving along Sheridan Road, minding my own business, whatever that means, when *wham,* I'm flooded with information from Everworld David.

All at once, enough craziness to make me swerve into oncoming traffic, almost kill the other driver and myself, which brought up the eternal question: If I died here, in the real world, would

Everworld David continue to live? And the other scenario, if I died in Everworld, would there still be a real-world David to drive this monster of a car?

Merlin, Neptune, a freak storm and shipwreck, April stepping in just in time to keep me from being skewered by a genuinely psychotic Roman god. Having to step in because I'd spoken stupidly, without thinking.

I slammed the steering wheel with the palms of my hands.

And then I saw her, suddenly, as if summoned by the sound of my hands hitting the wheel, as if waiting for her cue. Not one hundred percent sure at first, but as the car pulled out of a side road and swung into my lane, about three car-lengths ahead of me, I had no doubt it was her, the maid, the middle-aged lady I'd seen once before, just after another Everworld update. The short, chunky middle-aged lady who'd stood in the rain, ignoring the fact I'd just vomited in her driveway, or her employer's driveway, the black-eyed lady who'd asked me what message I brought. Asked me if the gateway had been opened. Told me to close it. Close it.

I'd told myself then that she was talking about the actual, physical, wrought iron gate at the foot of the driveway, not about Senna, the gateway between two worlds. I'd told myself the woman was just some superstitious soon-to-be-old lady from Poland or Mexico or someplace less sophisticated than the good old U. S. of A. I'd told myself that and not believed a word of it even for a minute.

And then, later, I'd mentioned part of that encounter to Jalil. I didn't plan on telling him and afterward wasn't sure I should have. I think I did it because Jalil is smart, his mind keen and focused on provable truths. He has no time for psychic phenomenon or uncertainties or what he would call primitive mumbo jumbo. . . . Well, he had no time, when we first crossed to Everworld.

Now, I'm not so sure Jalil hasn't made his own concessions to magic; we all have. But the point is, Jalil didn't seem to find my story all that interesting. I found that comforting. Knew I was telling myself lies but felt comforted all the same. If Jalil didn't think my encounter with the foreign lady was meaningful then it probably wasn't.

And yet, here she was again. Definitely her, though I wondered what the "maid" was doing driving a black Mercedes S Class with tinted glass.

Maybe I should find out. Follow her. Not

much choice anyway on Sheridan, which is two-lane.

Some guy in a Jag was crawling up my butt, looking to pass. I slowed down. I'd let him pass, let him get between me and the Mercedes. Didn't want to drive on her tail, wanted to seem innocent.

The Mercedes slowed. Matched my speed. I drew a shaky breath and told myself it was coincidence.

The Jag punched it and zoomed around both of us.

I glanced at my watch. Four-thirty in the afternoon. The sky was almost dark now, not quite, and the air had grown appreciably chillier. The top was down on my car and the cotton, button-down shirt I had on was not cutting it as protection against the evening air. Nice. In Everworld I was lucky to get a small piece of unmoldy bread a day to eat and have a rag of clothing to wear over my shivering butt. Here, in the real world, my body cried out for a sweatshirt, a jacket, a sweater, anything to keep my precious self toasty warm.

The Mercedes was pulling off the road, not an easy or safe thing to do on this narrow road, a road with no real shoulder. Why? She must have seen I was following her. I'd gotten too close, been too conspicuous. Had she recognized me? Had she just thought I was some creep and already called the cops on the car's cell phone?

I passed her, thought I'd better keep going, look innocent. But no. This had to happen. I had to know.

I pulled over, too, forty, maybe fifty yards ahead of her. Cut the engine and sat for a moment, wondering if she'd get out of her car, come to me, or if she'd pull out, engine racing, tires screaming, speed away.

Nothing. Almost two full minutes of nothing and that's too long to sit and wait. I got out of the car. Checked for traffic coming up my back, and walked slowly back toward the Mercedes. As I got closer, I realized the maid had cut her engine, was just sitting there. As I got closer still, the driver's-side window slowly slid down. My stomach sank and goose bumps rose on my arms. I was close enough now to speak.

"Ma'am? Is there some trouble with the car? Do you need help?"

Yeah, that was believable. Nothing weird here, lady. Just a helpful Boy Scout.

Definitely her. A squat, gray-haired, middle-aged lady in a black, shapeless dress and black baggy sweater. Hardly able to see over the steering wheel. She looked up at me, her dark eyes focused on mine, and I felt I couldn't pull away. Was she for me or against me? Would she enchant me, kill me, or help me? My hand reached of its own accord for a sword that wasn't there. She noticed the motion and revealed a faint smile.

"Have you closed the gateway, David?"

I shivered, hoped she didn't see that involuntary weakness, that bodily response to the cold evening air, only that. "I don't know what you're talking about, ma'am," I said, faking a slight, condescending smile, a polite teenager talking to a batty old woman.

She smiled back, a nonthreatening smile, probably calculated to put me at ease, to make me drop my guard. A strangely young smile.

"You are wise not to trust, David. Please, follow me to my home. I have much to discuss with you."

While we'd been talking, only a minute, evening had truly fallen. The sky was now charcoal, the temperature plummeted several degrees. Or had this woman meddled with the passing of time or with my perception of the passing of time? I was nervous, full of misgivings and questions, angry about being nervous. But I would follow her. It was better than living on and knowing nothing, letting this short, fat woman in black scare me.

"All right," I agreed, looking at her round, suddenly kindly face, now illuminated like a moon in the surrounding darkness. "I'll follow."

I did. I followed, wanting not to, wanting to overtake her car, pass on a two-lane road, dangerous but maybe not as dangerous as following her home. But I followed. After a few minutes, she turned into a long driveway. The gate opened automatically, just a sensor, not magic. Maybe. We approached the house I'd glimpsed last time but not really studied.

I wasn't surprised to see it was one of the fairly typical old-money, late-nineteenth-century homes that were common along this part of Lake Michigan. A house for a single family but built on a palatial scale to accommodate staff, guests, and, in those days, members of the extended family who came to stay. Elderly grandparents, tubercular sisters, ne'er-do-well cousins.

There was something dark and a bit forbidding about the house, though that feeling might have been caused or at least exacerbated by the weather and time of day. And by my being just generally creeped out. The house was made of stone, limestone, I think, weathered, and looked kind of like it could have been found in England. I counted four levels of windows aboveground, not including minuscule windows in a sort of turret on top.

Much of the building was covered with clinging, climbing ivy, which added to the sort of dark romance of the place. I could see no lights on above the ground or main floor, and even those seemed dimly lit.

The Mercedes's brake lights glowed and I pulled up behind her at the top of the driveway. She got out of her car and waited for me at the front door of the massive stone mansion. Waited while I put the top up on the Buick. It would be colder going home.

When I joined her, she turned and inserted a key into the lock. Wordlessly, I followed her inside, where she tossed the key on a small table in the foyer. *She's not the maid,* I realized.

We walked past a large, central, swooping staircase, built of some dark, gleaming wood, down a narrow hall floored with marble tile and lined with prints or paintings framed in gold, to the back of the first floor of the house, to the kitchen. It was something out of those home decorating magazines my mother was always leaving open around the house.

"Let me make you some tea," the woman said as I stood just inside the door, awkward, silent. She motioned toward the table and I walked over, sat in one of the chairs. I noticed the room was warm, not overheated, but cozy. In spite of my nervousness, I noted that.

"Thanks, but, I don't drink tea," I said, vaguely afraid of being poisoned or charmed or . . . *Caution, suspicion, be wary, David.*

She turned from the stove and smiled. "Well, then, something else hot? You look frozen in that thin shirt."

I shook my head, embarrassed. Noted now that this old Polish or Mexican woman had no accent. I mean, she'd had an accent, at first, but not anymore. "No, thanks."

She shrugged, completed making a small pot of tea for herself, slowly, deliberately, then joined me at the table. Took a sip, no milk, no sugar, then put the big white cup down in its sturdy saucer.

"I am Brigid," she said. Her eyes were on me again, watching, waiting.

It meant nothing to me, her name, her statement. Except that she didn't look like a Brigid, more like a Maria or a Sophie. I realized I was stereotyping, trying to get a grip.

"I thought you were the maid," I said, then realized, the moment the words were out of my mouth, I sounded rude. Suddenly, I didn't know what to do with my hands, folded them before me on the oak table, then put them in my lap, felt foolish, crossed my arms across my chest.

Brigid smiled. "You were meant to think that, David."

"How do you know my name?" I asked.

"I know many things," she answered, calmly taking another sip of the still-steaming tea. I was warmer now, being inside, but watching her drink from the large white ceramic cup made me wish I'd said yes to her offer. The room, with its cherry wood cabinets and tomato-soup-red walls, the steam rising from the tea, the long day, it had been a long day, school, an extra shift at Starbucks, filling in for a buddy, sitting here with this gray-haired woman, this grandmotherly type, this nice, dark-haired middle-aged lady . . .

"Could I . . ."

The steam from the tea cup, it was making my eyes blur, making me see things. I rubbed them, blinked, put my hands flat out on the table, closer to the woman, the young, red-haired woman, like April, like April's older sister, long, red hair but darker, less curly, eyes wiser, a few thin, spidery lines at the outer corners of her eyes, a gentle smile. But at the same time she was

growing larger, not huge, not monstrous, just two
feet taller than any woman should or could be.

"You're one of them," I said, feeling a heaviness deep down inside.

"Yes, David," she said. "I am Brigid. The goddess Brigid."

I jerked involuntarily, pushed against the table. The teacup fell over. Dark liquid spilled on the surface, dripped, *plop*, *plop*, *plop* over the edge, onto the tiled floor.

Still, she sat, this beautiful, slightly more mature, definitely larger version of April O'Brien. Looking at me, her face calm and lovely and serious, righting the fallen cup, mopping the mess with a napkin, pouring more tea from the small teapot on the table.

Then she smiled, April's kind but gently mocking smile. "You really must learn, David, not to be so impressed by what you see."

"You're here. In the real world."

"So I am. Drink, David," this new woman, this goddess said.

"Thanks anyway," I said and pushed the cup

away. I wouldn't put it past any god to poison someone. "Who are you?" I said. "What do you want?"

She took a sip of tea before speaking. "You have heard of the Daghdha," she said, as if knowing my answer.

"Yeah." I was not going to give her more.

"Killed, eaten by Ka Anor. His treasures in the possession of Nidhoggr, the dragon."

I nodded, missing my sword. Questions racing in circles around my brain: How did a god get into the real world? Had she been left behind when the others migrated to Everworld? And did she have all the powers of a god? If so, how?

"I am his daughter, the Daghdha's daughter," the woman went on.

"So?"

She smiled, unfazed. "So, to answer a few of the questions I see swarming in your brain, I am neither god nor human, just a poor shadow of my former self. I am trapped between two worlds, as are you. I am here and I am there; I can neither die nor truly live." Here Brigid smiled again, resigned. "It's a curse I brought upon myself, though, so there is no use in my bemoaning my fate."

Her words were meaningless, vague, tantalizing. What did she mean, trapped like me? I was

human. She was a god, a goddess maybe I was
supposed to call her. Either way, not like me.

"Why are you here, in this house? What are
you doing in this world?" I asked.

Another sip of the tea. *It must be cold now,* I
thought inanely.

"David," she began, "I have the gift of prophecy.
Long ago I knew the day would come when the
gateway would be born, a woman-child with the
power to pierce the barrier between worlds."

She paused and in spite of myself, I reached for
the cup of tea. She was going to too much trouble
just to kill me. And I was thirsty.

"I waited many centuries, David," she continued, her voice lower now, somehow older. She
was shrinking back to normal size. It almost
seemed as if the effort to assume her true size had
worn her out.

"All the while I grew weaker. Now, though they
may seem great to you, a human, my powers are,
in fact, almost gone. Finally, after all the years, finally I felt the mother's presence. Under my direction, certain friends chased this woman away,
chased her until she took refuge in Everworld,
with Isis, the Egyptian goddess of fertility. I
hoped she would be safe with Isis. Isis is wise."
Brigid paused again, stared at a spot of spilled tea
on the table as if she were reading its secrets. Like

it was a crystal ball and she were a two-bit gypsy at a county fair.

"So you found this woman," I said brusquely. Senna's mother. It had to be. "Your problem is solved. Why do you need me to close the gateway when you've already taken care of it?"

The god raised her eyes. Green, like April's, but darker. Shadowed. And almost disappointed. In me. As if she knew I knew there was far more to her story.

"There was a child, David. For a long time I didn't know that this woman had left a child behind, here in this world."

She leaned forward, toward me, reached for my hand now on the table. I withdrew it, sat back. Watched her decide to leave her hand outstretched.

"The child is dangerous, David," she said, her tone urgent, serious. "The child can bring untold chaos. Horrible destruction. You must stop her, David. You must."

I sat in that kitchen chair, the chair out of some architectural magazine, surrounded by expensive, stainless steel appliances, by thousands of dollars worth of early twenty-first-century domestic luxury, a room that had nothing, nothing to do with the insanity and grit and blood and magic of Everworld. I sat in that kitchen with a goddess of the ancient Celtic peoples. Unable to determine if the woman who sat across from me was friend or foe.

"What do you care what happens over there?" I said.

Brigid stood and walked to one of the floor-to-ceiling windows that faced out on an artfully lit patio. Probably a garden, a yard. Maybe a pool, tennis courts. Her back to me, she stared out into the late evening sky for a moment before turning. Crossing her arms over her breasts, her hands on her shoulders. Compelling me with her eyes, a tilted head, to listen.

"Stop her, David. Give her to Merlin if you can. He is great and wise, you must believe that. Kill her if you must. But stop her, David. Stop her."

I jumped from my seat, hands clenched into fists at my side, anger surging. Who was she to tell me what to do, to tell me to imprison Senna, kill Senna! That wasn't the fate Senna deserved. Prison, execution, neither was a right or fitting end for Senna. Senna the witch was selfish and cruel and manipulative but I would always love her, always try to protect her. So who was this woman, safe in this monument to material security and comfort, who was she to tell me, the one carrying Galahad's sword, the one in the trenches, what to do?

"Why the hell would I trust you? Why would I listen to any of you so-called gods? Bunch of psychos high on your own power, playing your own games and to hell with any dumb mortal who gets in the way. Why would I trust you?" But the woman by the window didn't answer my questions. The woman by the window simply began to shimmer.

"You are gone now, David. You are gone."

CHAPTER X

I was awake.

Jalil had taken second shift, Christopher third, but I'd woken and now I relieved him, less than halfway through his time.

After the encounter with Brigid I couldn't sleep again anyway. I lay now on a narrow, uncomfortable bed, staring at the ceiling I couldn't see in the dark, wondering why I insisted that we keep watch at all. What was I going to do if Neptune decided to take us out? The ocean pressed in around our fragile air bubble. A word from Neptune and we'd be dead, no argument, no struggle. Should I tell the others about Brigid? Not Senna. That much I was sure of. Not Senna.

I pressed my hands against my head and almost laughed at the silliness of the gesture. Like I was trying to wring out my brain. Too many questions. Too many unknowns. Too much thinking. Brigid. Merlin. Neptune.

Thinking, too, about the deal we'd made with the Coo-Hatch. Hoping nothing had gone wrong. Thinking if experience meant anything, something probably had. Thinking about getting out of this place and back to fulfilling my promise to Athena and the people of Olympus.

Ever since I first saw the city of Ka Anor, I'd thought about how to take him, the alien god, down. How to breach that obscene stronghold, that massive, five-mile crater of ragged, thrusting glass daggers. That monstrous hole in the middle of which stood what Christopher called the Junkie Dream Mountain, Ka Anor's hollow needle lair.

Artillery. If you had enough of it, if it was powerful enough, if you set up on the rim of the huge chasm, maybe you stood a chance of blowing the entire tower to kingdom come. Boom. With the Coo-Hatch cannon, I just might be able to do it.

Which just brought me back to the Coo-Hatch and Senna's mother and Brigid and Merlin and Olympus and round and round, and all the while I was helpless here at the bottom of the ocean.

Weird. I was obsessing over everything but my current predicament. The mind goes to things it can handle, I guess, and avoids the impossibilities. What next? I should be focusing on the here and now. What next from mad Neptune? He expected us to put on a show.

I laughed out loud. I should be planning an act. I laughed again and started giggling like an idiot. Forget Merlin and Brigid and Ka Anor and Olympus and the Coo-Hatch — hell, I had to rehearse!

My laughter was evidently a signal that we were awake, for right then the door opened and admitted a stunningly gorgeous, I'm-too-sexy-for-a-human, Salma Hayek look-alike mermaid who had just brought a platter of food to the door.

I kept my eyes down as I took the platter, thanked her. Maybe it was lunch and not breakfast, but the look of disdain on the mermaid's face made me not want to ask. Made it easier to lower my eyes and keep my mouth shut.

I turned around with the platter to find Christopher smiling a singles'-bar smile.

"Dude, she wants me. I can tell."

I laughed. I don't know why except that Christopher's ability to drive me crazy with his moaning and piss me off with his bad attitude was tempered at times by his ability to make equal fun of himself.

"Half beautiful woman, half cold fish," Christopher said. "Reminds me of someone." He batted his eyes at Senna.

If Senna even heard she gave no sign.

"You know, the thing is, it's polite when you're in a foreign country to adopt the local ways and customs," Christopher said, turning his attention to April.

"It just seems wrong for you to be all bundled up like that when clearly the polite thing to do would be to, you know . . ."

"Don't hold your breath." April, pushed her hair back off her face, yawned. "Though I'm not sure that means anything around here."

I put the platter on the table. "We should eat," I said. "No knowing when we'll get the chance again. I'll wake Jalil."

"I'm awake," Jalil said, joining us. "So what's going on in the real world with everyone? I aced a chem test, no big deal. My dad's got me sanding the floor in the dining room. Didn't see any of you alone, though."

"My parents had a small dinner party," April said, standing by the food, her back to her half sister. "Decided it was time to stop grieving over Senna's disappearance. They're talking about turning her bedroom into an at-home office for my dad. So we had a sort of mini-wake. We watched home videos."

Senna laughed derisively. "And there wasn't a moist eye in the house."

"Dad was actually a little emotional. He feels guilty. Me, I managed to keep my own feelings of grief and loss under control."

This tension between them, the deep dislike, distrust, maybe unmitigated hatred between April and Senna bothered me more than I let anyone know. At times it made me feel almost physically ill. In some ways it wasn't my business, just a family feud. In others, it was absolutely my business. I was the leader of this accidental team and there was dissension in the ranks. Could I trust either April or Senna to come through for the other in a time of crisis?

"Christopher?" I said, hoping he'd lighten the mood a bit.

"Not much. Stayed home from school one day, puking my guts up. Stomach virus, not fun. Called Jalil but his little sister, one of them, said he was out, SLAM! Good-bye, white boy."

Jalil shrugged. "Hmmm. That shows unusual good sense on her part. Tell you something interesting, though. That little creep, your little racist Nazi friend, what's his name?"

"You mean Keith?" Christopher asked.

"Yeah, the one who likes to point guns at people. Cops came by and asked me if I knew where he might be. Seems Keith has disappeared. Nowhere to be found."

Was it my imagination or did Senna look away a little too quickly? Imagination. Had to be. She wasn't involved with Keith. He was Christopher's problem.

"Disappeared?" Christopher narrowed his eyes. "What, they think you killed him or something? You? Why didn't they come ask me? If anyone was going to kill him, it would have been me. The little turd."

Jalil stroked his chin, a parody of thoughtfulness. "Let's see, why would the cops question me and not you? Hmmm, let me think deeply on that question. Why would some white cops harass me, a black guy, and not you, a white guy? By the way, did you kill Keith?"

"Yes, but I left behind a couple of Will Smith CDs to throw suspicion onto you."

"If anyone offed the littlest Nazi it was probably one of his own boys," Jalil said.

Christopher raised a glass from the food tray and held it high. "A toast to whoever disappeared Keith."

"A public service," Jalil agreed.

Christopher drank and spit. "Jeez! What the hell is this? Oh, my god, I think it's supposed to be beer. I've finally found the beer even I won't drink." He looked with distaste at the paltry platter of fish and greens. "I thought Romans were into gorging. I thought they knew how to live."

"We're not Romans," Jalil pointed out. "We're not one of them. They probably consider us some new type of beardless barbarians, slave material. Why waste good food on the scum?"

Christopher poked at a spongy yellow chunk. "Some kind of tofu. April, you're going to be happy here."

"What about you, David?" April asked.

"What?"

"You seem interested in what we've all been doing in the real world. What did you do there?"

I gave a guilty start. But I covered it with babble. "Nothing much. Work, school, errands for my mom, a minor skirmish with her boyfriend, the usual. It was a quick visit; I wasn't asleep long."

Then — the door behind me swung open. I spun around, sword out, ready. Just the merman who'd showed us to this house.

"Glorious Neptune is in the mood for entertainment. You will come with me now."

I hung back to walk with April. No breakfast that I could stomach, no clean clothes for the barbarians, hardly any sleep, a disturbing, real-world encounter with a beautiful goddess. And now, without preparation, we were supposed to put on a show for Neptune?

"April? What do you know of Brigid?"

"Who? Do I have a class with her?"

"No, not someone at school," I said testily. "I mean the Celtic goddess. Daughter of the Daghdha."

She grinned. Cocked her head, red curls, now mostly dry, tumbling to cover one shoulder. "Like Jalil was supposed to know all about ancient Africa and African gods? I'm Irish like five generations ago, David."

I sighed. Hadn't meant to offend her. Suddenly, I wondered if she still had any Advil left in her backpack — I had a headache. "No. Sorry, not like you're our resident Irish person. Like maybe a woman into feminist stuff knows something about the great goddesses, the mother figures."

April laughed. "Oh, that's better. Good cover, David. But yeah, I do know something. I think. I've been reading mythology books. Seemed like a good idea. Anyway, if she's who I think she is, she's some kind of triple god — you know, Creator, Preserver, and Destroyer. Birth, life, death. A lot to do with fertility. Childbirth. Healing, too. Poetry and inspiration. I don't know her story, though, what happened to her and all, if that's what you mean."

"Yeah, okay."

"Why? What made you ask about Brigid?"

April's question was innocent enough. My answer was not.

I shrugged. "I don't know. Name popped into my head. I must have read something once. No reason."

April gave me a long, suspicious look. She didn't believe me. But she decided to let it go with nothing more than a whispered, "Bull —"

CHAPTER
XI

We were led out of the house filled with air, back into the native watery environment. It was still a hard transition for me to make. There is something permanantly disturbing about breathing water.

April's long, thick, red hair and Senna's long, sleek, blond hair took flight again around their heads, dancing like copper and golden snakes, beautiful Medusas. Our clothes billowed and our steps became slow and exaggerated. We were five sad examples of John Cleese's Minister of Silly Walks from the old Monty Python days.

Back through the city the way we had come, to the reviewing stands, filled once again to capacity, humans hawking fish treats piled on large clamshells, Coo-Hatch huddled together in the aisles, looking like they'd rather be anywhere else, then back through the wall of shimmering water, back onto the floor of the arena.

This time, there was no horse race in progress, but several small, makeshift stages had been set up around the field of packed sand. On one stage, a fairy played a sort of mandolin as a satyr chased a nymph, then made an elaborate show of catching her. On another stage, a lone human male, dressed in a short skirt and knee-high strapped leather sandals not unlike what the Roman and Greek soldiers wore, juggled small ceramic pots. At his feet lay groups of other items for juggling, none of which I could see clearly.

I could also see now why he needed to be in an air pocket. One thing you don't do underwater is juggle.

On a stage close to Neptune's viewing throne, three mermen performed feats of strength. One wrestled what looked like a massive eel, another fought off the lumbering advances of a brutally big giant, the third hefted an Everworld version of barbells over his head. The center shaft looked suspiciously like a large timber from our sunken boat. At either end of the timber was attached a plate piled with a variety of skulls.

"You will wait here," our guide said, stopping

in front of the only unoccupied stage. "When Neptune commands it, you will perform."

The guy took off and we clambered soggily up onto the stage. All except Senna, who leaned against the structure, a little behind us.

Just then a watery roar came from the stands, a bellow or rage, no words, just out-of-control emotion.

Neptune. He jumped from his throne to his feet, stamped them up and down in a child's version of an Indian rain dance.

Pointed at the juggler, who stood frozen, trembling, one of the pots smashed at his feet. "You dropped one, you dropped one!" the god screamed, his face so red he looked like he was about to stroke out. "You're not supposed to drop one! Guards, kill him, kill him, then find me another juggler! No, let me, let me kill him!" Neptune's face broke into a wide grin. "I will do it!"

The juggler fell to his knees, just collapsed like a closed bellows, whimpered, brought his hands together in the popular gesture of supplication, of prayer. But he didn't offer a plea out loud, probably knew it didn't matter, his life was over, nothing he could say would reach Neptune. I wondered to what god the juggler was praying.

For a moment, it seemed nothing was happening. Neptune simply stared. But then the water began to form. A bubble of water around the man's legs, rising to his chest, up to his chin.

The man tried to run but the water bubble stayed with him. He stretched up on his toes, trying desperately to keep his mouth above water. Neptune laughed delightedly, and the water level rose another inch.

Water was now spilling into the man's open mouth. He gagged and spit and choked and Neptune let it go on, let it go on as the man tried jumping up to suck in a little air.

The juggler jumped, and every time he came down the water was higher. Higher. Now he could no longer jump. Now he could no longer reach the air. Now he strained, trying to force his head out the side of the bubble, but no good, the bubble moved with him.

He was drowning. Lungs filling. His face showed shock. He felt the water in his lungs, not the breathable water, the killing water. It was in his lungs, and he knew he was to die.

It wasn't quick. It seemed to go on forever.

I turned to look up at the reaction of the people in the stands. On the faces of humans, elves, even, I imagined, the Coo-Hatch — fear. A message received. On the faces of the mermen and mermaids, on Amphitrite and Triton —

hysteria. They shouted with laughter, pointed, slapped knees, wiped tears from their eyes. I turned back to the juggler. His face was bluish, his eyes seemed to bulge, his mouth worked like that of a fish just caught and thrown onto the floorboards of a rowboat.

When he was dead, the water evaporated. Neptune gestured for one of his mermen guards to haul the body away. The god sat back, well pleased with himself.

"I'll say it again, this guy is nuts," Christopher muttered. "I don't just mean like all the gods are nuts — this guy is a psycho."

"Persecution and murder as spectacle," Jalil murmured.

"All right," I said, shooting a glance at Senna, still leaning against the stage, her head in her hand, eyes closed. Safe enough. "Come on, what are we going to do for this maniac? April, songs?"

April just stared at me blankly. We were all pretty much at a loss.

"Christopher," I said, "can you think of something that will work for the Water Boy?"

Christopher shook his head. "I'll try, dude, but old Thorolf and his Viking posse were pussycats compared to this nutjob."

"*Try*, Christopher," April said. "I'll try to help you out if you get stuck. We all will."

Christopher shook his head. "Oh, yeah, that should help. Well, here goes nothing." He cleared his throat, another strange thing to see or experience while breathing water, took a step forward, and began singing to the tune of ". . . Baby One More Time." Yes. The song by Britney Spears.

"O, mighty Neptune, as far as the gods do go
you have the greatest power.
And mighty Neptune, we think all the world should know.
We'll shout it from the highest tower.
Glor-eee to the god of the sea, tell them all please
to bow down and respect him, oh, because . . ."

Jalil closed his eyes. "It was nice knowing you, April, David. We are chum. Fish food. Bait. History."

CHAPTER
XII

But Neptune, sick and childish Neptune, liked the song and demanded Christopher sing it again. And again. April joined in, hesitantly at first, but more aggressively when she saw Neptune smile and wink. None of us were above buying the god's favor, at least until he let us offstage.

And while we sang, me more mouthing the words than making any noise, I suddenly saw the sailor, the lone survivor of the shark attack, Merlin, walking slowly, slowly along the sidelines, Senna at his side. *Damn it,* I should have forced her up onstage when Neptune bellowed for a performance. Some weak, soft spot in me had decided to let her stay where she was, let her rest. Now I was losing her.

I couldn't break away, rush Merlin; Neptune

would kill me for ruining his personal party. Senna wouldn't go with Merlin willingly; she was under his spell. It was clear after the attempted kidnapping in Egypt, after the display with the self-powered boat, now this disguise, his leading Senna away, that Merlin had regained all of his strength after the monumentally losing battle with Loki, after failing to keep Galahad alive.

But Merlin wasn't going to get far with Senna, not if I could help it, and I would. Somehow. *Think, David.* Observe. The fact that they were moving so slowly, that they were walking so closely together, made me think maybe it was costing Merlin to keep Senna so completely under his thrall, especially while maintaining his own disguise.

I kept the wizard in my sight. And continued to play the performer. We segued to "Row, Row, Row Your Boat" sung in rounds. Neptune tried to get the hang of the rounds, coming in at the end of the first line with the beginning of the first line, but obviously this proved too much of a creative or intellectual challenge for him. And gods don't like to look foolish.

"Enough!" the god bellowed. "Enough of the songs. They begin to bore me. I want the fool, what is his name? Let him come forward! I have decided I would like to hear some amusing tales. I have decided I am in the mood to laugh."

April shot me a worried look. I froze. I could pretend to sing. I could pretend to dance. But being funny? That wasn't something I could do, not easily, anyway, not on command. I was no Dennis Miller, no Chris Rock, no Jerry Seinfeld.

"Life or death, David," Jalil whispered. "Think knock-knock jokes, anything."

"Hey," Christopher hissed, "why don't you recite him that poem you wrote for English that time? It cracked *me* up."

The others were not helping. And not one of them said anything about Senna's being no longer with them. Was it a part of Merlin's magic? Or just that they didn't care?

"Fool! Speak!" Neptune roared.

Think think think, David, you idiot, think! And then, I came up with a way to save Senna, stop Merlin — no matter what Brigid had urged me to do — and protect my own sorry butt.

I stepped forward, stumbling a little, still unused to the water's resistence, the need for exaggerated motions.

"Mighty Neptune!" I cried. Did my voice sound high and squeaky to anyone else? "I am David, a great wizard, and I will entertain you with amazing feats of magic!"

Neptune stared at me for a moment and then — laughed. A deep laugh, from the belly. Not what I'd expected.

Tears ran down his face, and he continued to laugh and laugh and laugh, pointing at me now, poking the lackeys beside him, forcing them to join in his mockery of me. My face burned or felt like it did. He was humiliating me. I was letting him. I couldn't turn around to see how April, Jalil, Christopher were reacting, couldn't look at Senna, hoped for once that Merlin's magic was blinding her to what was happening. I was mortified.

But I was also angry. My blood raced. I wanted to slice Neptune's sneering, jeering head off his neck and I could do it, too — with Galahad's sword I could do anything.

"Hoo, oh, whoo." Neptune was trying to regain his composure, wiping at his eyes with the back of his hand, taking deep breaths.

"You . . . he-he." The god forced his face into an expression of mock solemnity and seriousness. "You don't look like a great wizard. He-ho. Ahem."

Easy, David. This is not about you, it's about the big lunatic; he'd embarrass, maim, kill anyone, even his own mother; it's about his needing to show power, to step on necks, not about you. Not an attack on you. If you don't let it hurt, it won't.

I forced my face into a mask of theatrical dignity. My voice into a sort of pseudosophisticated, phony upper-class-British, AMC-classic-film tone.

"Mighty Neptune, appearances may be deceiving," I intoned. "I will prove to you that I am indeed a wizard of great power. Look!" I pointed dramatically at Merlin, in the guise of a young Greek sailor, one of our crew. "I will transform that youthful sailor into a wizened old man, before the eyes of everyone in this arena. With you, mighty Neptune, as my witness."

All eyes turned to stare at Merlin. Human, immortal, satyr, alien, dwarf, all turned to stare at the young, curly-haired Greek sailor standing next to the lovely gray-eyed, blond human girl.

Merlin met my eyes. It was an acknowledgment that he had lost, at least for now. I hoped it was an acknowledgment. He had to play along with me now; I'd trapped him, or we'd both be skewered.

Merlin was no fool. He nodded slightly, his lips forming a thin smile. A worthy adversary. He was going to go along with me.

I put my hand on the hilt of my sword. "Watch closely!" I commanded, jumping off the stage. "I am going to turn this sailor in the prime of his life into a feeble, decrepit old man!"

Again, Neptune laughed. This time, the laugh

was short and nasty. "None are so decrepit as the dead, wizard. I wish to see you turn this living mortal into a lifeless piece of ripped flesh and spilled blood. That is what I wish to see."

"David!" It was April, behind me, but what could she say or do to help? In Neptune's mind at least, maybe in the Roman mind in general, there obviously was a very fine line between comedy and violence. Between harmless goofing around and sheer brutality.

I didn't turn around. Instead, I stalked toward Merlin, who stepped away from Senna, almost as if to greet me. The person supposed to kill him. I couldn't imagine Neptune would change his mind at the last minute, issue a reprieve. Wasn't sure I wanted him to. Kill Merlin, or be killed by Neptune? A no-brainer. Kill Merlin, one less enemy, one less threat to Senna.

Close, closer I stepped, breasting my way through the weighty, watery atmosphere, until I was within ten, maybe twelve feet of Merlin. Until I could look into his eyes, the large brown eyes of a Greek boy on the verge of manhood. The body I was going to slaughter in cold blood.

"Your sword will not harm me, David," he said now, lips barely moving but the words were clear. "It was I who gave it to Galahad, I who wove the magic spells about it. You may try, but you will not succeed in harming me."

Relief warred with frustration. Defeated again. It would have been murder. It would have been mercy.

My sword. It wouldn't abandon me. I pulled on it. It didn't move, stayed nestled in its scabbard. What? Pulled again with more effort — maybe it was the strange environment that sapped my strength — yanked. Nothing.

Someone snickered.

One more try and yes, the sword came free. I lifted it, tried to lift it, grabbed the hilt with both hands, grunted, pulled, tugged it up to point straight out from my chest. I was panting.

And more and more people were beginning to laugh. Right, I was a comedy act, like an early Jerry Lewis movie where he's always stumbling and falling down and looking like a jerky marionette. My father used to watch those movies, Jerry Lewis and Dean Martin. I never understood the appeal and now here I was, doing a skit straight out of a Martin and Lewis classic.

Merlin stepped back. I tried to step forward but . . . was whirled in a three-sixty by the sword, like a beachcomber holding an out-of-control metal detector. I fell to my knees, hands still gripping the sword, tried to haul myself to my feet, stumbled, grunted, fighting the resisting sword. Hearing the laughter of the crowd growing, growing. And no sooner was I standing then the sword yanked me to the left, and I followed, running awkwardly, unable and unwilling to let go, stumbling when the sword suddenly changed directions, swung to the right.

Above the laughter of the hoi polloi, Neptune's plebeian, subservient people, I heard the god himself, roaring, screaming, slapping his knee. I was killing him, I ruled, me and my moron impersonation.

The sword swung me around again and again until now I was facing Merlin once more. And could see that Merlin had released his hold on Senna, saw her glide toward Jalil, Christopher, April, not because they were her friends but because they were where I would soon be and she would be safe. She hoped.

Okay, I thought, exhausted, furious, *all right, I'm not going to have to kill him now, not yet.* The sword immediately lost its independence and was my sword again, my weapon. I sheathed it.

"Excellent, wizard!" Neptune boomed. "I am well pleased. Now, come, lucky sailor, your life has been spared, come have a drink with me."

Fine, I was a great wizard but it was Merlin who was invited to hang with the god. Fine by me. More than fine.

I made my way back to the others, forgotten, at least for now, by a god in serious need of Prozac.

Chapter XIII

"David, we've got to get out of here," Senna said. Her eyes were wild, her voice strained. She'd been scared by the ease with which Merlin had almost taken her away. *More scared,* I thought, *than by his overblown effort in Egypt.*

"I know," I said. "Merlin will come for Senna again, as soon as he can."

"But the party's just getting going, man," Christopher argued. "What can it hurt to hang a bit? Plenty of gorgeous merwomen. Plenty of food and wine. And a vomitorium so when you've had just a little too much you can purge a little and start all over again."

Jalil shook his head. "Christopher? You don't even know what a vomitorium really is."

"A hurling room."

"No. A vomitory is an entrance, or exit, I suppose, cutting through the seats of a stadium. It's an architectural term. *Vomitorium*, Latin. It's a door, a passageway. . . ."

Christopher raised his eyebrows. "A gateway? So, Senna is a vomitorium? Jalil, you are just a wealth of useful information."

"Stop it!" I shouted. Senna's face was pale, her posture rigid.

"Ssshh!" April looked around nervously. "No one's paying attention to us — let's keep it that way, okay, boys? Look, I personally think we should just let Merlin take her."

Her. April could barely manage to say her half sister's name anymore. Senna was standing not six feet away from her and April was talking about her like she wasn't even there.

I didn't say anything.

"Sounds okay to me," Christopher said. "Senna goes with Merlin. Or we can just leave her here to take care of herself. She's an opportunist, she'll live. And then we haul ass out of here."

Jalil spoke. Didn't look at Senna when he did. "I can't believe I'm saying this, but I'm for taking Senna with us. What happens to her is not the issue, folks, Neptune's the issue. He's insane and dangerous. He makes Jeffrey Dahmer look as cute and cuddly as my little sister's Hello Kitty collection. He could be killing Merlin right now, for all we know. We get out now, however we can. Get back to Olympus. Take Senna with us."

"Okay," April said shortly. "But has anyone even started thinking about how we get out of here? How we get to the surface? And if we make it that far, then what? Swim a hundred miles to shore?"

"Oh ye of little faith," Senna mocked. It was an odd thing to say, especially to April. "David will get us out of here. He always has a plan. Don't you, David?"

She smiled and I thought, *What's her deal this time? She needs us to stay alive, free.*

"Maybe not always," I said, not taking the bait, directing my comment to the others. "But right now, yeah. At least the start of a plan."

"Speak on, MacDuff."

April widened her eyes. "Shakespeare? You, Christopher?"

"Always the persecution. Always the assumptions, the prejudice. I'm not exactly a huge sack of stupid, you know. I . . ."

I interrupted. "Did you all see those chariots, outside the arena, on the way down here? We find one, take it, maybe two, ride like crazy to the surface."

"Assuming we don't get killed by Neptune's boys in the process," Jalil said. "And that those rigs are more than capable of getting us to the surface. From what I saw, they're pulled by seagoing creatures. Dolphins, sea horses."

"Killer whales. And those huge sea turtles," April added.

"Want to make a bet they can't breathe air?" Jalil stopped, nodded thoughtfully. "Wait, what am I saying? We've met flying horses. And talking horses, so W.T.E. You never know. It's definitely worth a try."

Christopher shook his head. "Uh-uh. Did you see how fast those things were going? Of course, I don't know exactly because, hey, I've never lived underwater before! I don't quite get the rules."

Christopher nodded to Jalil. "You don't remember the other part of that little joyride Athena sent us on? Besides the talking horses? Remember that we were almost slammed and rattled to death by horses who seriously did not know the meaning of the word 'whoa.' I could barely handle a horse-drawn vehicle on land, and I'm used to land. Water is another story."

"It'll be easier here," I said. "Smoother ride."

"Unknown dangers," April added, undecided. "Loch Ness Monster, Creature from the Black Lagoon, Godzilla."

"I think Godzilla hangs off the coast of Japan, April," Jalil pointed out, allowing himself a small smile. "In the real world. In B-movies. Besides, do you have a better suggestion? Does anyone?"

"Do you know what a floater is, David?" Christopher asked suddenly. "Do you? Well, I'll tell you. It's a body that's been drowned and left in the water for hours or days. It's black and putrified and bloated and damn near unrecognizable as human. We came way too close to being floaters when Neptune had his little temper tantrum. No more. I, for one, would like to leave a good-looking corpse. Especially if I'm going to be dying young, which I'm pretty sure I'm going to be doing."

"Then it's settled?" I said. "Let's go hijack some chariots."

CHAPTER
XIV

It wasn't hard to find the stables. For one thing, we followed the kind of pleasant smell of hay. Not really hay, of course, but some sort of seaweed Neptune's stable boys fed their charges. The stables were spotless, we saw that soon enough, but still, they smelled like any real-world horse farm.

Point to note: We could smell, our noses were working underwater, as well as if we'd been on land.

W.T.E. Again.

That's when we spotted a chariot with a broken wheel limping its way toward a huge, high-ceilinged, simply constructed building of white stone that dominated the surrounding area of Neptune's city. We took a chance and followed.

We followed it, knees raised high with each

step, legs thrust out as far as possible, used our arms in a breaststroke motion, moved as quickly as we could through the water. No one stopped us, no one questioned us.

The driver of the damaged chariot abandoned the vehicle at the wide double doors of the stable and handed the reins to a human boy who proceeded to lead the two medium-sized turtles and their chariot to a smaller, ancillary building, long and low.

"So, General MacArthur, sir?" Christopher whispered. "Now what? Like, if we run into any really large mermen on guard duty?"

"I think it's pretty obvious," Jalil said. "We knock them out. Correction. Davideus knocks them out with the flat of his sword."

Which is what I did. It was the only way.

April and Senna walked right up to Arnold Schwarzenegger and his equally large friend and started to flirt. It took a few minutes for the tactic to work. Both girls are attractive, I'll admit, in my opinion above average, though in very, very different ways — April is the sun and Senna is the shadowed moon. But compared to the mermaids we'd seen, and given the merpeople's obviously well-fed egos, these guys had to be coaxed into paying attention to Earth women.

But it worked and while the big mermen were

chatting, Christopher, Jalil, and I snuck around and behind. I nailed Arnold and they each grabbed one of the other's arms. Quickly, I motioned for April and Senna to look for someplace to tie them to. Not like we could tie their feet together. They didn't have feet. When Arnold and friend were bound and gagged and Jalil affirmed that the coast was clear, we headed farther into the huge stables.

The central space of the building was about the size of a commercial airline airplane hangar. In that space, in discrete areas, were parked chariots, piles of wheelwright equipment, and various workstations.

Along three of the walls were stalls, some more than ten feet across, for the numerous sea creatures in Neptune's service. The floors of the stalls were covered with thick layers of scattered vegetation, for warmth and comfort. Each stall had a feeding trough made of some nonporous material I didn't recognize.

As Jalil had said, the place was empty of people, alien or human or legend. No stable hands. Maybe it was lunchtime, break time, maybe the stable hands were off celebrating with their buddies in the arena. In any case, good luck for us, something there was way too little of in Everworld.

In some of the stalls, eating or sleeping, were the animals used to pull Neptune's chariots. Massive sea horses with thick, regally arched necks, absurdly tiny, translucent wings or flippers at their sides. Sea horses in bright fluorescent colors like fuchsia, acid green, hot orange, brilliant yellow. Dolphins, much larger than their real-world counterparts, gleamed in their shiny silver skins. A hot-pink giant squid, tentacles pure white, the suction devices that lined them scarlet. Impossible.

And then there were the chariots. Maybe about fifty in all. All large, though some larger than others. Made of bronze with silver trim and what looked like traces of gold on the scenes sculpted on the chariots' high fronts. Several were also encrusted with jewels, mainly pearls, or bits of sea glass in translucent blue and green and slivers of opalescent shell. A few were elaborately painted inside, with scenes of Neptune's real or imagined adventures, both amorous and military. Maybe not military, exactly, but scenes definitely involving Neptune shish-kebabbing someone.

It was an amazing place. Horse racing is not my thing, I mean sportswise. I'm a sailor, and though there's racing in sailing, I like more the discipline of sailing, the solitary or near-solitary nature of being alone or almost alone on an expansive body of water, just you, the boat, the water, and the sky. But there was no staying in this stable the size of an airplane hangar without feeling some of the excitement of the competition, the venerable — and debauched — history of chariot racing and magnificent animals bred for speed.

Of course, I was assuming the variety of creatures in this stable had been bred for speed, were the thoroughbreds of their species, but frankly, it was hard to believe that about, say, the massive sea turtles. So, maybe some of these guys had been bred for intelligence, for tricking the arrogant athletes out of the win, the assumed victory. Maybe.

Several chariots were ready to roll, animals already strapped up with harnesses and reins.

"Which chariot do we snag?"

"You mean, steal," April said.

"Okay, steal." Christopher rolled his eyes.

"We'll need two. They're not big enough to hold the five of us." *And,* I thought, *if we just take one it definitely lessens the chances of all of us getting out.*

Jalil pointed to the nearest chariot. "How about, *not* that one." Four turtles were already harnessed and hitched. They were easily eight feet long from blunt snout to notched tail, maybe five feet across at the widest part of their shell.

Their four legs were as thick around as three-gallon jugs and ended in dense, built-up toenails, each the size of a man's fist, toenails that would put a ratty old man to shame. Looks can be deceiving, I knew that maybe better than anyone, but these turtles just didn't look fast and we didn't have a whole lot of guaranteed positives on our side.

I nodded. "Right. We need speed, power. Okay, Jalil, Christopher, April, you three take the chariot at the far end of this row. Six dolphins."

I paused, assessed the other vehicles. "Senna and I will take the one next to it. Two giant sea horses. Let's hope they're half as fast as that four-legged horse Neptune's so in love with."

"Yeah, that wasn't too weird," Christopher said, giving an exaggerated shudder.

"Be careful, David." Jalil climbed up into his chariot, reached a hand down to help April. Looked back to me, nodded almost imperceptibly toward Senna.

He might have been genuinely worried about me, or, after all this time, still just wary, distrustful of my loyalties, but he wasn't offering to change places. No one was. Not that I would have let them. Back in Egypt I'd called Senna a pain in the ass to her face. And she was, always taunting and riling and tempting the others, the classic troublemaker.

"Speaking of dying an agonizing premature death," Christopher said brightly, squeezing in next to Jalil and April, "Should we just bust out of this stable and head straight up? What's the signal for up? What do you do with the reins to make the animals go up? Forward, I get. Right, left, no problem. Reverse — I'd figure it out. But up?"

I shrugged. "I don't know. But we're gonna find out."

"Wait." I focused on the wall that was to our left. Squinted to bring what I hoped I was seeing into focus. *Yes.* I jumped from the chariot. "There, against that wall. Christopher, Jalil, each of you, get out and grab one of those javelins."

They got out. April, still in the chariot, raised her eyebrows. "Uh, hello? What about me? I should go unarmed, sit around waiting for some man — and I use the term loosely — to protect me?"

Christopher grinned. "Ouch."

I followed Christopher and Jalil to that row of metal-tipped javelins. Spoke over my shoulder as I went. "If you think you can throw that thing and do some serious damage, be my guest. Senna

what about you?" I asked as I carried my javelin
back to the chariot.

"I'll pass," Senna replied smugly.

I held the long, slim, throwing spear at my
side, the bottom of the shaft resting on the
ground. The javelin stood at least a foot above my
head.

"Okay, here we go," I said, wedging the javelin
between me and the front of the chariot.

Without so much as a flick on the reins, the sea
horses moved slowly toward one of the walls of
the stable building. The dolphins with their chariot followed.

"Uh, chief? I'm getting the impression these
fishies aren't so bright," Christopher said from
behind us. "A few sandwiches short of a picnic.
Shouldn't they be moving toward, I don't know,
the *open* door?"

And that was the last word I heard because just
then the wall disappeared, simply shimmered out
of sight and with breathtaking acceleration that
made my head snap back and Senna fall on her
butt, the two giant sea horses took off.

It was unbelievable. A complete rush, like we
were in a rocket ship, not a two-wheeled vehicle.
I had no idea how fast sea horses in the real world
could move, but there was no way any real-world

animal, on land or in the sea, could match the instantaneous speed of these creatures. Not an alley cat leaping from the lid of a garbage can after a rat. Not a greyhound out of the gate. Not even a cheetah powering after a gazelle.

We flew out of the stable building, up into the air that was no air but water, out of the city, away from the arena, the colosseum. My hair swept back from my forehead, Senna's streamed like a flag behind her. My eyes widened against the rush of water, my throat worked, gulped, struggled to remember it was okay to breath.

"Woo-hoo!" Christopher, laughing, in the chariot behind us. "What a ride!"

"Where are we going?" April shouted as the second chariot drew abreast of ours.

"Out of here," I called. Away from here, away from Neptune's arena of blood and guts. Then, up to the surface. To dry land. Hopefully.

We hadn't even left the city behind when we heard the noise. The mournful, hauntingly beautiful, high-pitched cries of . . . I turned my head. Killer whales. A matched set, shiny black-and-white, pulling a much larger chariot than ours. Two mermen, one at the reins, the other hoisting something up onto his shoulder . . .

"Senna, get down!"

I yanked her to the floor of the chariot, dropped over her, still holding the reins, the javelin. The trident whizzed by, missing one of our sea horses by inches. The sea horse screamed, a strange sound like that of a wounded horse on helium.

"There's . . . six of them, David!" Jalil cried. "Six chariots, how do we outrun them, man?! These guys actually know how to ride!"

He was right. The mermen, two per chariot, were experienced hunters, madly blowing conch shells like a call to the chase, and we were the pitiful little foxes, doomed to run until exhaustion made us drop, doomed to have our tails cut off and paraded through the city. We couldn't outrun them. Their chariots, pulled by killer whales and yeah, the turtles, were superfast. I should have known, paid attention to reverse logic. Had to stop them some other way. Could we exhaust them? Probably not before exhausting ourselves and our animals.

Stop thinking, David, and just go! No point in using the javelins now. No way could we take good aim, hit a target while moving at this speed into unknown territory.

"David, look!"

I saw. It looked like a tunnel, like a narrow entrance to a cave. Tear inside and what? Meet a dead end, be trapped and taken? Or maybe find a path to the surface? No, stay in wide-open spaces. Only a fool would back himself into a corner for safety.

Another trident hit our chariot with a heavy clatter. The mermen didn't share Neptune's excellent aim but still, too close.

And then, I got it. Only a fool . . . Neptune's mermen thought everyone but themselves fools.

"Jalil, follow me, make it look like you're going through the tunnel. Veer off to the right at the last minute — do you hear me, the last possible minute. I'll go left. When I give the word."

Were our sea horses and dolphins traveling at top speed? Were we moving too fast to pull off the feint? Would we crash and burn? No, not if I could help it. "Senna, look back. Tell me how close the chariots are to one another, to us."

Cautiously, Senna peered around my legs. "I can't tell the distance," she admitted. "But there's more space between us and them than between their six chariots. They're in a kind of bunch."

Good. The mermen's arrogance was going to convince them that we were stupid enough to trap ourselves in a dark, narrow, and unknown space. They were going to follow us in — or die trying.

Closer now, closer. Hair streaming, sea creatures and coral formations rushing by, everything a blur. My hands tightened on the reins and I glanced over at the others. "Jalil, drop back and pull in tight behind me."

I saw Jalil yank on the reins, the dolphins jerk back, then to the left to get in place. Jalil was good, better than he thought.

This just might work.

Only yards ahead. My hands could sense the sea horses' reluctance to continue straight on into that looming black hole. Instinct, survival. But this was only going to work if it looked convincing.

"They're still coming, David," Senna cried. "Jalil's right behind us."

Closer. Only thirty, twenty, ten . . . "Go!" I shouted, wrenched the reins to the left, muscles straining with the effort of guiding the sea horses through the too-tight turn.

"They made it," Senna reported. "Jalil's gone off to the right."

And then we heard it. Chariots smashing, mermen shouting, animals shrieking. Our sea horses were on a solid path now, racing to the left at a forty-five-degree angle to the tunnel entrance. So I risked a glance over my shoulder.

Yes. A five-chariot pileup, just at the entrance

to the tunnel. Only the last chariot had escaped the crash, the merman at the reins trying frantically to back up the two massive turtles pulling his rig, cursing, screaming at his weapon man to keep his eyes on us.

We were free. For now.

CHAPTER
XVI

We traveled on, Jalil and I within sight of each other, and headed in the same direction. Still racing at what seemed like top speed. I didn't know how long the sea horses or dolphins could keep the pace. Hope we'd be far, far away from Neptune and his henchmen before the animals got tired.

And then . . . above us, the surface of the ocean! It had to be, I could see sunlight dully glowing through the skin of the water. If we could reach the surface before the mermen — what then? Closer to our own turf, would we have the advantage?

Up up up. I chanced a look over my shoulder. Yeah, one chariot was still coming. Even if I hadn't seen the mermen, I could hear the mad honking of their conch shells. Safe to say the sole survivors of the crash were pissed.

Up up up until . . . Finally, we broke through the surface of the water, like those synchronized swimmers, neatly and cleanly, with hardly a splash. Shimmering droplets of water fell gracefully from Senna's face and streamed off the backs of the sea horses as the chariot arced through the air several feet above the gently waving water before landing smoothly on the surface.

On the surface. Unbelievably, the sea horses speeded their way across the surface of the water, their tails and most of their lower bodies submerged, the bottom few inches of our chariot's wheels also beneath the water.

Then, several yards to the right and ahead of us, out of our direct path, the other chariot breasted through the ocean's surface, its dolphins leaping even higher into the air before settling back half-beneath the water.

"Wooo-hooo!"

I looked ahead to see Christopher grinning, arms up over his head. Jalil, back tense, hands clenched around the reins. April, facing backward, gripping the right and left rim of the chariot walls, her face a confused mask of excitement and panic.

I didn't answer. Yeah, it was cool, but how did we keep the chariots from descending again? How did we direct our sea horses and dolphins not back to Neptune's playhouse for perverted psycho killers but onward, toward land? And in what direction would we find land, anyway?

"Christopher is such an idiot!" Senna spit out the words like a bad taste. "We haven't lost the mermen; nothing's changed."

I didn't respond. Partly because at that very moment the pursuing chariot of mermen burst up from beneath the surface of the water exactly halfway between our chariot and Jalil's.

Senna dropped to the floor. It was now or never. In the split seconds it would take for the turtles to land, for the chariot to right itself on the surface of the water, for the mermen to orient themselves, we could strike. It was a long shot, we could easily screw up the chance to attack, but right then, it was our only shot.

"Christopher, Jalil, April! The javelins!"

I didn't look to see if they'd heard me. If someone had taken the reins, picked up the spears, taken aim. Senna and I were behind the mermen, but we weren't going to be for long. I flicked the reins, made a sound I hoped meant "go!" and for whatever bizarre reason, the sea horses went. Fast.

"Senna, grab the reins," I said, yanking her to her feet. "Don't move, don't change directions, just stand there, and for god's sake, don't let go!"

And in the time it took Senna to grasp the reins with wet, shaky hands, Jalil threw his javelin. He must have because I saw one merman slam backward in the chariot — and then watched as his body, a metal-tipped spear protruding from his chest, slipped out the open back end and under the wavelets.

One down. But I was close enough now. "Christopher, hold off!" I shouted. "Senna, bring us closer in!" While the surviving merman struggled to keep hold of the reins, process the fact that he'd lost his weapon man, and needed to grab for the guy's trident, I unsheathed my sword. Climbed easily onto the rim of my chariot and jumped into the merman's chariot.

He felt my landing, of course. He whipped around, snarling, furious that some lowly human had the nerve to attack one of Neptune's elite. With one hand still on the reins he grabbed for the trident. And I stuck my sword through his stomach.

I don't think he expected it. I don't think he'd even seen my sword. Stunned, he looked down at the sword embedded in his gut. Looked back up at me, uncomprehending. I yanked the sword free and the merman crumpled.

"Nice throwing, Jalil," I said.

He nodded. It wasn't the first time he'd speared

someone trying to spear him first. "I know it sucks, man. What we have to do in this place really stinks."

April had given the reins to Christopher. She glared at me but said nothing.

We were at a relative standstill. As still as you can be on the ocean, where drifting is simply what happens.

"I always seem to be asking you this, Davideus Maximus," Christopher said with a grin. "But — now what?"

Neptune's animals answered for us. Before I could open my mouth to say, "I don't know," the sea horses and dolphins dove, taking us with them.

CHAPTER
XVII

We'd gotten rid of the mermen, at least temporarily. Good news. We were back under the surface of the ocean, which was less good news. But as far as we could tell, we were still heading away from Neptune's city.

The sea horses powered on until about a hundred yards ahead I saw something that looked like a cave. Maybe more like a grotto, kind of pretty, with small geysers bubbling up from the ground just outside the cave's mouth. A lush variety of vegetation adorned the outside walls of the cave itself. A patch of hot-pink and mint-green coral formations, like stalagmites, created an exotic garden slightly to the left of the cave's mouth.

We were going to pass this place on the right, in a few short minutes, when . . .

"Whoa!"

The sea horses reared, screamed shrilly, yanked to the left in an almost sixty-degree angle. The chariot tipped, I slammed into the low left wall, Senna crashed into me from the right, slipped off her feet. I fought the reins, tried to bring the team back on a straight-ahead course, afraid they were going to try to double back, afraid we'd run right into Neptune, but they refused to respond.

And then I saw why. Emerging from the cave, causing the roof to crash in around it, was a — well, I don't really know what it was. But it was big. And ugly.

"Scylla!" Senna shouted over the continued screaming of the sea horses.

"What the hell is it?"

"Don't you remember what Neptune said? A weak, lustful man and a vengeful woman," Senna said into my ear and the tone of her voice was like a needle piercing my eardrum. "Scylla was a beautiful sea nymph. Poseidon, the Greek version of Neptune, maybe Neptune, too, wanted her. Amphitrite found out and put magic herbs in Scylla's bath. They turned her into this monster. She doesn't want me, David," Senna added, her voice slightly mocking. "She only eats men."

For about a second I felt bad for the once-lovely sea nymph. This thing, Scylla, was hideous. But I didn't feel so bad that I was going to sacrifice myself to her hunger for male flesh.

It was disgusting, suffering from mange, fur missing in patches, skin scaly and red. It stood on twelve feet, monstrous distortions of a dog's paws. Six massive, brutal-eyed canine heads sprouted on long, strong, hairy necks. Stringy drool and foam the color of pus spilled and bubbled from each mouth, each snarling mouth with its three rows of daggerlike teeth. The stench from the thing reached my nose and I tasted vomit.

And in the time it took for me to register these visual features, she leaped for us.

"Go go go!" I yelled to the sea horses, flapping the reins, thinking better to run into Neptune and go down fighting than to be snatched up in one of those dripping canine jaws of the hell hound. Had to get out of here. Had to warn Jalil, Christopher, April. But where were they? Somewhere behind us.

"Senna, take over!" I thrust the reins into her hands, and she didn't seem so cool and mocking now. "Hang on, don't let them break away."

A wave of foul breath smacked us. Senna gagged. The beast was close, Neptune's sea horses

no match against a vengeful monster lusting for
male flesh and blood. I yanked my sword from
my scabbard and whirled around to face Scylla.

With one leap she would be on us, on me,
jagged, bloodstained teeth closing around my
face. I lifted my sword and slashed with everything I had, severing one of the beast's heads. It
fell away but Scylla came on as if she hadn't even
noticed the decapitation, didn't notice the blood
spewing, pumping from the open wound. Still
Scylla came after us, extending the next neck and
head. Again, I slashed. This time the sword got
stuck on something tough and stringy, cartilage
maybe, and I yanked violently to release it. The
sword came out but the head stayed on the neck,
attached by only a few bloody strings, flapping
obscenely against the side of the neck.

This wound seemed to surprise the beast, slow
it down just a little, just enough for me to grab
the reins back from Senna and with one hand
fight fight fight against the sea horses' instinct to
run blindly, force them to turn back closer to our
original course, urge them on to greater speed.

"David, it's still coming!"

I looked over my shoulder. Scylla was enraged,
still in pursuit but slightly off balance with two of
her six heads missing.

"What have you done to my lovely?!"

The voice was unmistakable. Neptune. He'd obviously seen her wounded. But instead of coming after us, Neptune drew his massive golden chariot to a stop and called to Scylla, who went immediately to his side to be comforted. Neptune bellowed and cried and fussed over the bleeding dog-monster. Briefly, I wondered if Scylla's heads would grow back and decided I didn't want to stay around to find out.

XVIII

Relief. We'd outrun and outsmarted Neptune's posse and his pet hellhound. And now, from the right, from around an outcropping of rock, came April, Christopher, and Jalil in their chariot. One of the dolphins had been wounded but the five others were valiantly struggling to make up for their teammate's disability.

"Where the hell were you!" I shouted. "Everyone okay?"

Christopher stuck a thumb in the air. Water. They steered their chariot closer to ours.

Now, coming into view . . . something new, another terror or something that was much more benign?

Another city. Stunning, brightly lit, recognizably Greek in style and design, though with its own individual character.

I had no desire to stop by and play tourist. But I could wonder. Note that the city was enclosed by a large bubble that — yeah, every thirty seconds or so burped out a far smaller bubble, the size maybe of one of the new Volkswagen Bugs, which billowed toward the surface.

I looked over at Jalil, close enough now to speak, sea horses and dolphins slowed to a civilized pace.

"Air geysers," he said. "Has to be. Air geysers spewing oxygen, keeping the big bubble permanently inflated. The people in this place breathe air."

"Something else is going on," April said, squinting. "I think. Look closely at the surface of the bubble."

I did. "Yeah, a net of some sort. Superfine, silvery. Holds the bubble in place? The net's maybe tied down somewhere. What's it made of?"

"I think the bigger question," Christopher said, "is: Who lives here? And are they going to start firing some weird weapon at us in a minute?"

"I . . ." I threw my hands up over my ears, reins against my face, closed my eyes against the aural assault, fought to keep the sea horses from bolting, overturning the chariot. . . .

Neptune had found us. Of course.

His roar of demented, triumphant laughter reverberated through my body, making my heart race. Blood seeped from the dolphins' eyes, the sea horses' nostrils. It was louder than anything we'd heard from him before, like the screeching of subway car brakes, the crashing of fifty sets of cymbals, the crack of a sky full of thunder, a garage full of screaming car alarms, the wail of twenty-five fire engine sirens — all at once, sounding five feet away from our eardrums.

Too close, he'd gotten too close, I hadn't even noticed, too wrapped up playing sightseer. I managed to open my mouth, yell, "Go!" couldn't even hear my own voice, how could the animals, the others. I pulled my hands from my ears, winced at the pain, flapped the reins and the sea horses, in agony, bolted forward, toward the silver-netted city. Anywhere but here, had to get farther away from the source of the sound, maybe then . . . what what what!

Closer to the air dome, Senna crouched in the bottom of the chariot, head buried under her arms. Jalil, Christopher, April racing along with us, Christopher at the reins now, head scrunched down into his shoulders, mouth a grimace. April and Jalil poster kids for excruciating pain, clutching their heads, doubled over. Both teams of animals trailing blood.

Faster faster . . . when, suddenly, it stopped. Just stopped, in the middle of a riff, of a note, like someone had just hit the stop button on a CD player, just over, gone. Silence.

And in the beat it took my addled brain to register *silence*, it also registered *no air. Can't breathe, David, you can't breathe*. Neptune has cut off your magical ability to breathe underwater. Okay.

Senna's head shot up, she looked at me, eyes wide, mouth beginning to work, to try and find air, to suck in air through the water. . . . Frantically, I shook my head, and she choked, closed her mouth, opened it to spit out water but it's not so easy to spit out water in water, under the water.

Hadn't known the end of the air supply was near, hadn't known to suck in a deep lungful, had been too busy running away from the horrible noise, how long could I last? Get to the surface, try to get to the surface!

Even as my brain was giving itself instructions, it was failing, if I lived, if I . . . glanced at the other chariot, April hanging limp over a side,

Jalil, eyes wide, running his hand up and down his throat, Christopher . . .

My lungs were burning, my vision blurring to black to nothing, but not before I saw or maybe I imagined a silvery net, very pretty, unlacing, opening for me, how nice . . .

CHAPTER
XIX

"Whoa . . ." The mini cup of espresso launched itself from my hand, went smashing to the floor. Quickly, I knelt down to clean up the mess.

I was at work. Starbucks. Valued employee. Green apron. I looked up at the chalkboard behind the cash register. Today's special: some exotic tea-and-fruit drink I couldn't even pronounce. It was Saturday. Of what week, what month, didn't matter, didn't care. The Everworld me didn't, anyway. The Everworld me . . . drowning, had just crashed a chariot pulled by giant sea horses through an even more giant bubble enclosing an underwater city. Did real-world David care what day it was? Had he ever?

"David, I need a favor." It was one of my coworkers, Heather, unemployed actress. Nice enough. "A customer wants two pounds of

French roast. There's none up here but I know we got a box the other day. Can you go to the basement and get some?"

Can I? Sure. I can do almost anything. You wouldn't believe what I can do, what I can force myself to do. Could I, would I?

"Yeah, sure," I said. At least the errand would get me out of this overly lit monument to the marketing phenomenon of branding for a few minutes. At least I could be alone.

I headed for the basement. And not for the first time asked myself what I was doing here hawking designer lollipops and mood-inducing CDs and more types of hot and cold coffee drinks than any reasonable human, let alone caffeine addict, needed in a lifetime. What was I doing here, heating milk, stirring foam, grinding beans, hauling boxes, when I was needed somewhere else to do a far more important job not just anyone could do? I believed that last part. I . . .

One eye, just one eye at a time, David. You're awake now, you can open your eyes. Go ahead.

I did, opened them both at the same time, sat up, felt the tip of the soldier's spear against my breastbone. Okay. Slowly looked up to see the soldier's face, not cruel, just blandly doing his job. He was dressed in upper-body armor, a short, skirtlike toga thing, and sandals. At his side was belted a sword. On his head, a helmet adorned with a long spray of three feathers. A uniform very similar to those of the Greek soldiers we'd fought alongside on Mount Olympus.

Slowly, carefully, I turned my head, mostly slid my eyes to either side, to see if we were all together. We were. In a wet, bedraggled heap, surrounded by a total of four, maybe five guards, I couldn't look behind me. Someone's foot in my back, someone's arm under my thigh. Automatically, I jerked forward to slide off but the spear didn't move with me. It nicked my skin.

"Sorry," I said, hands in the air, nowhere near my sword. "I'm just sitting on my friend here. Can I move a bit to the left?"

The guard nodded and pulled the spear back an inch or two. I moved. Carefully. Looked to see that it was Christopher's arm I'd been squashing.

One by one the others tumbled to consciousness.

"Lovely. Another situation," Christopher whispered. "Ow, my arm hurts."

"Uh, sir, can we get up now?" I asked.

Again my guard nodded. The five guards — I saw there were five when I stood, shakily — stepped back but not far enough to allow us a path of escape. However, they didn't take my sword from me. Arrogance? Some sign of civilization? Or just reasonable confidence? At least two of the guards carried a bow and quiver of arrows, along with a sword or spear. Whatever the reason, I was happy to have my own weapon.

My guard spoke. "You are under arrest for illegal entry into the city of Atlantis," he said. Unaccented English, imagine that.

"Atlantis? You know," Christopher commented brightly, "all that's missing here is Buffy and Angel. And that little yellow Pokémon, what's-his-name. I mean, right?"

"You will come with us to the city council," the guard went on, "where you will present your case before the mayor."

Whatever flicker of hope that word brought was immediately eliminated by a thunderous boom that shook us all, guards, too, almost off our feet. It lasted less than a minute. Which is actually a very long time to be vibrating off your feet.

"What happened?!" April cried.

My guard spoke. "An earthquake, only one of the hundreds Atlantis experiences every year. Neptune and Poseidon are not known as the Earth-Shakers for nothing. They will go off now and annoy each other a while longer. Leave us alone, until next time."

"This dude is made to live in L.A.," Christopher said, hand on his stomach. "Me, I feel nauseous."

"And I'm seeing double," April said, blinking hard.

"Neptune and Poseidon," the guard explained as we watched the two similar-featured gods in their similar chariots make a macho show of thrusting and lunging at each other with their tridents. "Roman and Greek gods of the sea. The bearded one is Poseidon. For as long as anyone can recall, the two gods have been warring for control over our fair city."

"How do you withstand the attacks?" I asked, just as an aftershock rumbled through the ground below. "How do you keep them away?"

The guard allowed a small grin of pride to cross his lips.

"Monsieur Mayor Jean-Claude LeMieux."

XX

I'm sure just about every person over the age of six has heard of Atlantis, the famed underwater city. Or maybe it was a city built on Earth that for some reason sank, I can't remember. Doesn't matter. And it seems to me I've seen and heard lots of different descriptions of the city, in movies, in books, even, when I was a kid, in some comic book a friend lent me. I don't remember what kind of comic it was, I've never been into them.

So my head was full of vague preconceived notions, none of which came really close to the reality of Atlantis, or, at least, the reality of Everworld Atlantis. This was no small group of plastic structures stuck into the blue pebbles on the bottom of a fish tank.

The city was large but not immense, with a

dense downtown and a few sprawling suburbs. The main city was similar to the style and feel of Olympus. In other words, Greek. Except in far more normal proportions. The buildings were made from a whitish marble and the streets were paved with a similar stone. Both were well lit but the source of the light eluded me. Near what seemed to be the center of the city was a temple, a close replica, as far as I could tell, of the temple to Zeus or Athena at the Acropolis in Athens. There was also a discernible marketplace, teeming with rows and rows of stalls, close-packed, opposing storefronts maybe only ten feet apart. An agora. I'd picked up that term in Olympus.

We were taken to the city council building.

The building was a lot like the others, but taller, faced with an arcade of Ionic columns and above that, a pediment. In this triangular space were Greek letters. Later I found out they spelled out: *Liberty, Justice, Equality.* Clearly a building of public importance.

The room in which we gathered to meet with Mayor Jean-Claude LeMieux was grand but simple. The walls were made of what I guessed to be white marble, here and there lightly streaked with gray. The ceiling was — and it was hard to tell because the room had to be at least twelve feet high — painted white, whitewashed. The floor was also marble, pinkish. On the walls, at evenly spaced intervals, hung sconces and in those sconces burned oil lamps. The result was a largish room made intimate by a warm and rosy glow.

The mayor's staff person motioned us to take seats in a group of chairs arranged to be conducive for conversation. They were in a sort of cluster, not a neat circle, no chair enough behind another so as to exclude its inhabitant from the view of all or to make anyone feel like he was sitting in the second tier or cheap seats at a ball game. Among the ten or so armless but comfortable-looking, red velvet cushioned chairs was a larger, armchair with a high back, placed so as to be somehow central without being smack in the center.

Definitely the chair for the mayor or maybe, on occasion, for a visiting dignitary. If dignitaries in Everworld ever sat down to a civil conversation instead of simply killing off a few hapless bystanders. This larger chair was also upholstered in velvet, but unlike the others, the velvet was brocaded. I think that's the term, maybe it's "figured." I should know by now, what with those decorating magazines my mother reads and endlessly talks about.

There was no other furniture in the room, except for a small, simple side table against one wall. The room was sparse without being cold, elegant without being off-putting.

Of course, appearances mean nothing, especially in Everworld. For all I knew, LeMieux could come busting into the room astride a Bengal tiger, aiming a bow and arrow at my heart.

"It's pretty," April said. "Not my personal taste, I'm more into the French-country-house look, but nice. Odd that it's so European, not all ancient and Mediterranean . . ."

"Must have been some surface trading going on at one point," Jalil said. "Personally, I'd like it better," he added, voice grim, "if there were a few big, wide-open windows we could hurl ourselves through should the need arise to leave in a hurry."

"Isn't Atlantis just your kind of place, Jalil?" Senna said, her voice low, almost sultry. "Clean and orderly and . . ."

"It's more the kind of place we all like," April shot back. "Except you. I mean, we've actually been arrested or at least detained on specific charges. We violated specific laws. Before this, the closest we've come to real-world society is the fairy land market, monument to capitalism. Here, we've got the monument to fair government, government by the people, for the people. Democracy. Equal representation. Something you'd know nothing about."

"Don't make assumptions, April," Jalil said quietly. "I'm hoping for a jury of my peers, too, but this is Everworld. We can't forget that."

We sat, me gravitating to the chair closest to and just to the right of the large one, LeMieux's. To my immediate right, Senna. Grouped to LeMieux's left and completing a sort of crude circle, April, Jalil, Christopher.

The straight-backed, no-armed chair allowed my sword to hang at my side, in easy reach.

We waited. Not that long, but the five or so minutes seemed like forever. I was on guard, suspicious, like Jalil, not completely soothed by the notion of finally having encountered a somewhat democratic society. Too many risk factors, too many ways everything could go bad on us. Again.

Besides, it's not like me to think everything's going to be just fine.

Finally, the door at the far end of the room opened. In walked a smallish man, not six feet, trim, though given his age — sixty-five, maybe seventy or more — looking a little scrawny. He wore a sort of modified toga, more modest than the one Dionysus had worn. Somehow, long, loose sleeves had been sewn onto the garment, as well as a similar sort of leggings. There was an air of dignity about the man, though not one of arrogance. The mayor. Following him was a much younger man, someone I assumed to be a member of the mayor's staff.

The mayor and his companion approached us. We stood, a trained reaction to the presence of someone with a title. The man acknowledged us with a general nod and sat in the large chair. The staff member lifted a chair away from the group, sat, and opened a file of papers.

"Please." The mayor gestured for us to sit.

"From where have you come?" LeMieux asked. His manner was gracious but formal in the way of all politicians. No mention of the fact that we had broken a law of the city and were in that room against our will. There was no need for him to remind us who was in charge. And he knew that.

"There's an interesting answer to that question, Mr. Mayor." Christopher paused. "Would you like the full or abbreviated story?"

"Sir," I said, before the man could answer, "Mr. Mayor, we apologize for arriving in Atlantis illegally. We were on our way to the surface, from Neptune's, uh, place, but we had a little trouble."

The mayor gave a small smile. "There is always trouble where Neptune is concerned. But where did you come from before that, for something

tells me you are not native to these parts. And
you may call me Monsieur LeMieux."

"Okay, Monsieur LeMieux. We're from the old
world. Or the real world, sometimes we call it
that. Most recently, though, we've been helping
Zeus and Athena defend Olympus against Ka
Anor's Hetwan forces."

The information seemed to take the old man
by surprise. For a minute I thought I'd screwed up
again, that, of course, this guy was affiliated with
the Romans, an enemy of the Greek gods and
people. And then the mayor of Atlantis rocked
our world.

"Then I am truly pleased to meet you," he said.
"For I, too, am from what you call the real
world."

CHAPTER

XXI

I literally sat on the edge of my chair as LeMieux told us his story. Only Senna seemed carefully uninterested but I knew better.

"It was the early 1960s, maybe sixty-two, maybe sixty-three, I cannot now remember exactly. I was, at that time, how do you say . . ." The old man gave a slight shrug. "I was involved in activities that would not have been sanctioned by my government or that of the United States."

"You were a spy," Jalil said, brain working rapid-fire, as usual. "For who? Had to be the Russians, back then. Cold War."

"Yes, yes, the Russians. You see, I had been operating a somewhat small and only marginally lucrative smuggling operation in the South Seas. Certain illegal substances. On the rare occasion, weapons. However, before long it became clear to me that my business was not growing and perhaps in danger of being subsumed by more powerful men than me, groups of men, organized groups with more money, better boats, more connections."

"So, you decided to betray your country?" I said.

April shot me a look.

LeMieux wasn't offended. "What was my country doing for me, at that moment? Nothing." He smiled at me in a way that reminded me of one of my dad's older Navy buddies, a guy who whenever I was around him always made me feel impossibly young and ignorant but, strangely, not too bad about it. Like, it wasn't a crime to be young. Like, I would be old soon enough and wise.

"Besides, the LeMieux you see here today is not one hundred percent the LeMieux of yesteryear. Much has happened since that time. Much has changed."

"So, what went down?" Christopher said. "How did you get to bizarro-world? I'm not going to believe you came willingly."

LeMieux shook his head. "No, no, not willingly. One of my first assignments for the Russians was to observe various preliminary activities and collect information regarding an above-ground nuclear test. Planned and scheduled by the Americans."

The old man paused.

"Is it difficult to talk about what happened?" April asked sympathetically. I saw Senna roll her eyes.

"Not any longer," LeMieux replied. I believed him. "I am just struggling to remember. It all seems so long ago, so part of a far-off world, as if it all happened to another LeMieux, not the man you see before you. Here is what I recall. A particular night, the sea was rough. I prided myself on being a good and seasoned sailor, but accidents happen, eh? Sometimes, one is simply a victim of circumstance."

He wasn't speaking to me personally, but I nodded. Yeah, accidents happened. Yeah, circumstances could make you a victim.

"Perhaps I was at fault, perhaps not, perhaps it was the bad weather. Perhaps God had other plans for me than being a petty smuggler and spy. Regardless, my boat capsized. Vaguely now I recall being trapped beneath the hull, freezing, no doubt dying, drifting slowly but certainly closer to the site of the scheduled blast. And then —" LeMieux raised his hands together and then spread them in two arcs. "An explosion of light unlike anything I could have imagined. I thought I was dead, at the gates of heaven. But I was not dead."

Again, LeMieux paused. Shook his head. "What happened next," he went on slowly, "was extraordinary. It was as if . . . as if the world had been turned inside out, its skin, what we ordinarily see, ripped open, flipped over to expose the dark underside. I had been under the boat, but now, somehow I was free of it, floating free, in or above the water I could not tell. And that is how I saw the sky peel apart and the clouds twist and churn. And my own body." LeMieux frowned. "My own body also wrong. I looked at my hand and saw not flesh but bone and muscle and veins. I could not bear to look anymore, after that one horrible sight."

We all knew. Christopher, April, Jalil, and I knew. We all remembered that early gray morning at the lake. The old man's words had brought it all alive, brutally alive again for us, the universe opening, inverting, turning inside out, sky boiling, the monstrous wolf rising from the water.

Christopher looked ready to blurt something out. I shook my head. I'm not sure why, except that something made me not want the old man to know we'd experienced the same sort of passage. His coming across had been, it seemed, an accident. Ours, I think we all believed, had not. It occurred to me then that I wasn't even sure if Senna knew what had happened to us, exactly. I didn't even know what it had been like for her, crossing. Had never thought to ask.

I looked at her now. Her face was still carefully expressionless. For a split second, a fraction of a second, I wished she would look at me and smile. But I knew that wouldn't change anything.

LeMieux went on. "When I woke, for it seems that at some point I lost consciousness, my boat had been righted. Quickly I climbed aboard, only to be almost immediately surrounded by what I recognized as sailing ships of the ancient world."

"Who were they?" April asked.

"Atlantean surface sailors," LeMieux explained. "They carried me down to Atlantis in a diving bell that runs along a great rope suspended from a floating platform." LeMieux turned to me. "This was almost forty years ago, but the diving bell is still in use today."

"You were taken prisoner?" Jalil said.

LeMieux seemed to consider his answer before speaking. "No, not really," he said. "Atlantean society was too fractured for anything so civilized as a fully functioning judicial and penal system. You see, at that time, the fair city of Atlantis was in a dreadful, sorry state, on the brink of civil war, in fact. The people were divided into two main factions, though small splinter groups, fanatics mostly, also wielded some influence over the people's thinking. One major group claimed loyalty to Neptune, Roman god. The other, to Neptune's archrival, the Greek Poseidon. Here were the residents of this independent city begging to be ruled by one of two despotic gods. This made no sense to me."

I nodded. It made no sense to me, either, or, I'm sure, to the others. Except maybe to Senna. Possibly she would welcome a group of willing slaves.

LeMieux went on. "Poseidon was demanding extortionate tribute. Neptune was threatening to destroy the city unless it paid tribute to him. And the citizens of Atlantis were killing one another for the privilege of being slave to one god and victim to the other. No one had the time to bother with a stranded sailor from the old world. So . . ." Le Mieux smiled, a wise, self-satisfied smile. "So I decided to seize the opportunity I saw before me. I decided to end the internal strife. I decided to remake myself in the image of a leader far more democratic than either already on the ballot, to prove to the people of my new home that I was the man they wanted to lead their city. Not Neptune or Poseidon, not some other despotic god. But a true politician, something the Atlanteans had never known or encountered. Someone they could not defend against."

Christopher leaned forward. "How did you do it?"

"The details are boring," LeMieux said, with a small show of false humility. "Suffice it to say that by establishing myself first as a hardworking citizen, and then by putting into effect the time-honored politician's skills of bribery, cajolery, manipulation . . ."

"Bad press on the opponent, baby kissing, smear campaigns, unfounded accusations, the art of the deal, lying," Jalil added.

LeMieux bowed his head. "As you wish. But over time I became the most respected man in the city, trusted by all factions, given the responsibility through a general election — at the suggestion of one of my most loyal supporters — of heading up a central government intent upon keeping troublemaking immortals at bay."

"It's what we've seen all over Everworld," I said. "Plenty of violence and lunacy, but very little skepticism, hardly any cynicism. No one questioned your motives in taking power, did they?"

LeMieux admitted this was so. "My rise to power was uncontested. At least by the Atlanteans. Neptune and Poseidon were, at first, puzzled by my tactics, by my audacity. However, the same innocence, if it can be called that, exists in the gods as in the mortals, and before long I was forging a treaty with Poseidon while playing Neptune off the Greek god to keep his demands from becoming unreasonable. With the two gods more occupied in the checking and balancing of each other's power, I was free to establish for the first time in remembered Atlantean history a healthy economy based on the harvesting of fish, shellfish, and even a quantity of gold for sale to surface-dwellers. And thus you find us today, a well-ordered, economically strong society."

"What happens . . ." April stopped, her face flushed. "I mean, do you have a son or a daughter? A protégé?"

LeMieux chuckled. "Death is not something one can avoid, or something one should not talk about in polite conversation," he said. "It is not a taboo subject. My death is a reality I admit each and every day. And," he said, looking from face to face, "it does worry me to think what will happen to my Atlantis when I am gone. I have tried to train one or two men, native Atlanteans, Everworlders, over the years, yet whatever strengths they possessed were overshadowed by their profound and seemingly unchangeable naïveté."

LeMieux sighed. "In the meantime, it is good the gods should be fighting, Neptune warring with his rival Poseidon. For in this way, their attention is focused away from Atlantis and on each other. And I can still hope to find among the city council staff a worthy successor to my position as mayor of Atlantis."

CHAPTER
XXII

"Monsieur LeMieux, have other people from the real world, the old world, crossed into Everworld?" April asked.

The old man shook his head. "I do not know," he admitted. "Perhaps. It is no longer of great concern to me, to seek out such people. I have made a life here, in Atlantis."

"Would you like to know about our world, as it is now?" April asked. "I mean, I'm not a historian or scholar or anything, but I could tell you some things."

The old man smiled. It was a kind smile, almost pitying, too.

"No," he said, placing his hand over April's. "I do not wish to know anything. It has been too long. But I thank you, young lady, for your offer."

"Well, what about the opposite?" Christopher pressed. "Like, have you ever tried to get back to the real world? To your old life?"

"Yes, long ago, I tried, thinking perhaps there was a physical path somewhere, somehow, leading to the surface and then . . ." LeMieux shrugged. "There was not."

"You say you don't want to know what's happened to the world since 1963," Jalil said, his voice sharp. "That means you haven't been back, ever. That you don't cross when you sleep. That you don't cross over to the real world. You have no presence there. You're just not there anymore. Or, maybe, you are there, still, and here."

"No." LeMieux sounded surprised. Interested. "No, I have never gone back. I have always assumed I was dead to that world, a missing person. But I do not know for certain, of course. Why do you ask this?"

"We cross," I said. "When we sleep here, we sort of wake up back there. I mean, all the while we're awake here, we're living our normal lives back there, eating, going to school, sleeping, going to work. There are two of us, or one in two parts, or something like that. But when we go to sleep here, it's like the us back in the real world gets this sudden update. The two of us merge. We suddenly know or remember, our brains or memories suddenly tell us what's been going on over here. To us. In Everworld."

"That must be very disturbing," the old man commented. "I am glad I do not experience such a thing. If there is another . . . another LeMieux back there, on the other side, I do not think I want to know about him."

"Yeah, well, schizophrenics are us," Christopher said with a laugh.

All of a sudden Brigid came to mind. Brigid the shape-shifting Celtic no-longer-god, not-quite-human I'd met twice now in the real world. A god didn't necessarily need a physical pathway to travel from one world to the next. I knew that much. Was Brigid an Everworlder who had crossed back to the real world? A god who had taken up residence, if it could be called that, in Everworld only to leave, to cross the barrier back to the real world — forever? Is that what she meant by being trapped between two worlds? Had she ever crossed to Everworld at all? She'd said she'd made a decision. Had she refused to leave the old world? Why?

"Monsieur LeMieux," I said. "You tried to escape Everworld and failed. Do you know of anyone else who has succesfully escaped? Who maybe has traveled back and forth?"

"Do I know of one who has accomplished such a feat?" he repeated. "No. But, of course, there is talk, there are rumors. It is said that from time to time, when, no one can predict, a person of unique powers is born. A person who is a passageway, a gateway. Through that special person, one can travel back and forth, from one world to the other." Again, the old man shrugged.

Don't look at Senna, David, don't give her away. I said to myself and silently willed the others not to give Senna away, not to say, *Well, Mr. LeMieux, this is your lucky day, meet Senna Wales.*

Nobody spoke. The old man went on. "However, such an occasion, such a person is rare. Failing his — or her — presence, it is said that the only way it is possible for one to accomplish such travel is to rewrite the Great Scroll of the Gods."

"The what?" Christopher asked.

"The Great Scroll of the Gods. Again, there are rumors. It is said that this document is a plan devised long ago by the chief or father gods. In it they charted a map of Everworld, detailed its substance, stated its laws."

"The software!" Jalil said excitedly. "I knew it. I knew it all along."

I flashed a look at Senna. Her face was pinched with curiosity; she couldn't hide her interest any longer. And I thought of Brigid again. And the jist of what she'd said: *Close the gateway, David. Kill her if you have to. The dark ones are close.*

"Where is it?" I demanded. "Where is the scroll? Who has it?"

"No one knows," LeMieux admitted. "At least, if there is someone who knows the whereabouts of this scroll, his — or her — identity is a secret. You see, the Great Scroll was hidden from all, even from its creators, so that no one could ever attempt either to destroy or to own it. To manipulate it to his own selfish ends. Because you see, of course, that whoever is in possession of the Great Scroll could alter it in such a way as to change its very essence, could rewrite it to serve his own will. Could even rewrite the very existence of Everworld. Now you see why it is so important that the document be well hidden and protected."

Christopher ran a hand through his hair. "Holy crap. That just might be the best news I've heard all day. All day? What am I saying? Since I landed in this looney bin."

"The best news assuming we can find the Great Scroll," April added. Then shut her mouth when she saw LeMieux's worried frown.

"We're not after the scroll," I said quickly. "What we want to do is get back to Olympus."

And what I want to do, I thought, *is hope the*

others weren't thinking what I was thinking. That the best place to hide a document so dangerous, so potentially world-altering, universe-shattering, would be beyond the bounds of that world, that universe. In the real world.

With Brigid?

Trying to look like I wasn't, I glanced at Jalil. He was the one I had to be most wary of. He was the thinker, the self-server, probably my friend, yes, but Senna's tolerant enemy.

I had mentioned Brigid to him. Once. I hadn't told him everything, nothing about my second encounter with her, but what would it take for Jalil to deduce the location of the scroll, enlist the others, find the scroll, maybe Brigid would help him, use it to kill Senna, destroy Everworld . . . where would I be then? Who would I be then?

I met Jalil's eyes. I hadn't meant to. They were narrowed, snake-slitted, knowing.

The member of the mayor's staff who'd accompanied the mayor into the room approached with a sheaf of papers and asked for a moment of his time. LeMieux turned away to speak to the man.

"Do you know what this means?" Senna grabbed my arm, squeezed, her eyes glittery with excitement.

"What?" I knew, was pretty sure I knew what her answer would be, but I asked anyway.

"The scroll, it's what I've been hoping for. It would give me total, complete, absolute power over this place, over Everworld." She bared her teeth.

"Now, that is a surprise, those words coming from Senna's mouth. You really should shoot higher in life, Senna. Dictator, is that all you want to be? You're just not meeting your potential," Christopher said.

"I'm thinking something different," Jalil said now, quietly. "I'm thinking that scroll could be used for a good cause. Nothing to do with Senna's personal desire for domination. Hey, magic software, no problem. I can handle it. Software is software."

"Okay look, no one's going after the scroll. The goal here, right now, the immediate goal, is to get back to Olympus. To help Zeus and his pitiful little army of humans fight off the Hetwan."

"Isn't this secret piece of paper of any interest to you, oh mighty Davideus?" Christopher asked, eyes wide.

"Of course." If he only knew of how much interest. I could save Everworld. I could save Senna. We could go home. It could be done. We had been told so. "All I'm saying is that first things first, we get back to Athena."

"Your protectress." Senna, sneering.

I acted like I didn't care.

"Quiet. Here comes LeMieux."

The old man had finished with whatever business he'd had to attend to and rejoined us.

"Sir, Monsieur LeMieux," I said, "can you help us escape Atlantis? Get past Neptune and Poseidon and back to Olympus?"

The mayor hesitated. Maybe our enthusiasm about finding the Great Scroll had made him wary of our real intentions. Probably.

"If we succeed and Olympus is saved," I went on, "we'll demand that Zeus intervene to protect your city, Atlantis, in the future."

LeMieux smiled wryly. "You have the ear of mighty Zeus? From what I understand, he is not much more, shall we say, reasonable, than his brother."

"We have the ear of Athena," I said. I could easily imagine what sort of comment Christopher was struggling not to make. Yeah, and he'd like another part, too. . . .

Another moment passed before the mayor answered. "I will help you, my new friends, but I cannot guarantee your safety. The gods, Neptune and Poseidon, are angrier than ever before. Their might is great. They have many creatures and other, less obvious powers of destruction under their command. Now, come with me. We will dine first, then I will send you on your way."

"So, we're looking at what, a dinner of Oysters Rockefeller, Lobster Newburg, Clams Casino? Maybe a little champagne to start, a dry white wine to finish?"

LeMieux looked at Christopher with amusement. "I am afraid we survive on more simple fare. But the quality of the fish is superb. It far surpasses anything to be found in the common fish markets of the old world."

Christopher made a face. "I knew it. Sushi."

CHAPTER XXIII

After dinner, the first decent meal we'd had since the food we'd been given by thankful villagers on our trip down the Nile, LeMieux led us out of the city council building and through the streets of Atlantis.

While we walked, April and the others chatting with the mayor, Senna walking silently beside me, my thoughts wandered. Went back to the strange moment of silence that had followed LeMieux's mention of his frustration at being unable to find a worthy successor. Went back to everyone's eyes on me. In expectation? Suspicion?

Someday, LeMieux would be unable to govern. He knew that, acknowledged that someday soon he would fall sick and die. Atlantis would need a

new mayor, a man of wisdom and courage, a wise
warrior. Could that man be me?

It could be me. Or not.

I'll try to be worthy of your sword.

I'll try.

I'd said that, promised that to Sir Galahad, the
perfect knight, as he lay under a pile of stones
we'd pulled together and layered on top of his in-
cinerated body.

And right now, it seemed, the job in front of
me was to learn how to operate a rickety old diving bell. If you even operated a diving bell and
didn't just sit in one waiting to die.

Christopher barked a laugh. "Okay. I'm just
saying no."

It was laughable. It looked like something out
of an old black-and-white silent film about the
nineteenth century, a thing without any refer-
ence to twentieth-century technology, something from *The Perils of Pauline,* something a
helpless heroine in a frilly pink dress might
find herself trapped in by an elegantly thin,
mustache-twirling villain bent on compromising
her virtue.

April cleared her throat. "Well, it is kind of . . .
pretty."

Okay, the diving bell was beautiful, in a very,
very old-fashioned way. It was made of a shiny

metal, which I seriously hoped was steel, and decorated all over with lacy gold patterns. Each stud that connected each sheet of shiny metal to another was inlaid with mother-of-pearl. But . . .

"It's just so small," Jalil muttered. "Like a Porta Potti. Like a little elevator but . . ." He peered through one of the small windows. "But with no controls. It's a dumbwaiter. It probably leaks. I don't understand . . ."

I turned to LeMieux. "Not that we're not grateful," I said, "but are you sure this, er, thing, is going to get us to the surface? It looks kind of, well, old."

LeMieux shrugged. "There are risks, as I have told you. But there is no other way I can help you reach the light of day."

I looked at the others, one by one. Saw the resignation on their faces, even on Senna's. "Then, let's go."

We took our leave of the mayor of Atlantis. Promised again that we would try to enlist Zeus's help as protector of the underwater city. Unspoken caveat: If we survived.

We crammed ourselves into the diving bell. An Atlantean soldier closed the door behind us. And slowly, slowly the chamber began to rise along the thick, coiled rope that extended from Atlantis to the surface of the ocean.

We ascended, April watching the beautiful underwater city disappear below us, Jalil's mouth set in a tight line, Christopher, unbelievably, humming "Row, row, row your boat," Senna — silent.

Approximately ten minutes had passed when I felt the first, small tug. Then the diving bell lurched to one side and we tumbled with it, arms outstretched to break falls, knees slamming against the floor, the five of us now piled into one lump, too shocked, too caught off guard even to scream.

Jalil craned his neck toward one of the small windows. "Oh man, oh man, it's a shark!" he cried. "It's biting through the ropes . . ."

"We're going to sink!" Christopher yelled.

"No, we're not, we're going to shoot to the surface!"

And then — it was like being on one of those amusement park rides that yank you straight straight up only to drop you straight straight down just as suddenly. But we weren't going to drop, just continue to shoot wildly to the surface like a rocket.

I braced myself against the wall of the diving bell as best I could. Fought the panic. "Decompression!" I said. "We're going to get the bends."

Jalil shook his head, like the mad racing of this chamber of horrors wasn't enough for him, he had to further shake it up. "No. Think, David. Unless the chief gods wrote something in the Great Scroll, it doesn't exist in Everworld. You ask me, I think they know diddly-squat about atmospheric pressure, any rules of science."

"You'd so better be right," Christopher wailed. And then vomited. "Sorry, man, can't help it."

And then, the diving bell lurched to a stop. Not a complete stop, now we seemed to be rolling. Light flooded through one of the small, water-spattered windows. Dimmed, then shone through again. We'd broken through to the surface. The diving bell continued to bob like a cork on the waves, but at least the mad ascent had stopped. We could see sky for a second, then water, then sky again. Maybe it was all right, maybe we'd make it out of this alive. The question now: How to steer this thing to land. The more important prequestion: Could it even be steered?

"Oh, no," April whispered. "Listen!"

I did. And heard through the walls of the diving bell the familiar roar of Neptune's enraged voice. Close. Closer.

Then . . . another voice, deeper but just as enraged. Neptune and Poseidon. A contest of vocal wills. Trading insults. Bellowing wordlessly.

"The boys are at it again," Christopher said

weakly, still looking a little green. "If they see us, we're goners."

Jalil lifted his face to a window. "I'm betting Neptune's forgotten all about us already. Which doesn't mean we aren't going to be in the way. Which doesn't mean we aren't going to die."

It started. A hurricane, two hurricanes, whipped up instantaneously by the competing gods of the sea. Gale-force winds, twenty-foot waves. And our diving bell was just a random piece of flotsam caught in the mother of all macho displays of immortal testosterone.

We were in a washing machine on the spin cycle.

We were battered and bruised and bloody. Fingers poked into eyes and feet pounded into guts. I clutched my sword as tightly to my body as I could to prevent anyone but myself from being sliced apart. Jalil's head slammed into one of the windows and left a smear of blood. Senna's pale face was gray. One of her hands hung strangely from her wrist. Probably broken. April's bottom lip was torn open where she'd bit down on it. A line of blood trickled from Christopher's left temple.

We wouldn't last much longer, injuries mounting, stomachs emptying. And when the gods stopped raging, when the sea calmed down again . . . what then? Would we simply float, bob peacefully along the surface of the ocean, a pretty antique diving bell with five dead bodies inside? Five teenagers dead of internal injuries, dehydration, starvation, take your pick.

And then, like magic the violent heaving of the waters stopped, just stopped. And with it, the mad motion of the diving bell. The chamber was filled with groans and sobs and Christopher's favorite mantra, "holy crap holy crap holy crap." Now that we'd stopped being thrown around like an old beach ball, we had time to cry and wail.

Just enough time to cry and wail, for April to wimper and pray, for Christopher to curse, for Jalil to mutter to himself, think his way calm, for Senna to close herself off completely from me, jerk away from my touch, wrap her arms around her frail battered body.

Just enough time before the diving bell, our pretty little prison, was shoved up on the shore.

CHAPTER
XXIV

We climbed out, pushing, tumbling, everyone crawling to a space of sand all to his or her self. Glad not to be up close and personal with one another, glad to be alone for a minute or two, to retch, lay a warm cheek on the cool sand, close eyes too weary to stay open.

After a moment I sat up. Looked around. This was not Egypt. And it wasn't anywhere near flat-topped Mount Olympus, either. No mountains of any sort in sight.

The others, struggling to sit up, Jalil to stand, stretch, Senna on her back, eyes open, arms widespread, looking too like an offering to a god, like she'd looked in the mouths of Sobek's croco-diles, staring at the sun.

I used my sword to help me stand, leaned on

it, grateful for it. We'd find shelter, take some time to rest before . . .

"David!"

I whirled. April, she was to my left, now backing away slowly toward the ocean, her eyes wide, her face upturned.

"Holy . . ." Christopher scrambled on all fours, sand spraying up behind him, then leaped to his feet, turned his back to the water.

Jalil grabbed one of Senna's arms, pulled her roughly to her knees, dragged her until she got to her feet, spitting mad.

Then she saw. We all did. How could we not have seen! Had we been that sick tumbling from the diving bell, or had this giant thing just appeared, taken one huge step from the other side of this place and *boom*! landed here?

I could say it was a giant but it was nothing like the few giants we'd seen in Neptune's arena. This thing dwarfed those giants, it dwarfed Loki in one of his expansive rages, made Zeus in his thunderous phase look as harmless and insignificant as a toy kids get at Burger King.

It was at least, I don't know, thirty, forty feet tall. I could see that its face, though far away above me, was hideous, both because it was so big and because it was genuinely ugly, all out of proportion to be human, but still vaguely human, like the face of someone who'd been in a terrible car accident and patched back together by druggie freaks.

The nose was — not there. There were two cavernous, oval-shaped holes flat against the face. We were looking inside bone, at the place where the skeleton would join the cartilage and skin and whatever else makes up a human nose. Like the giant's nose had been neatly torn off and then tossed away. No plastic surgeons in Everworld to replace it.

The mouth was lipless, the gums partly eaten away, showing all the rotting teeth to their roots. The teeth seemed too big for the mouth, like a grizzly's teeth in a human baby's mouth, as if maybe even with lips the giant couldn't have closed them over the teeth.

One eye was sunken down below the cheekbone, as if the socket had simply melted and slid and taken the eye with it. The other eye, bright red where a human's would have been white, was where it should have been on a human face but lacked an upper lid. How? The eye couldn't blink, just bulged and stared and gave the impression it was going to fall, *plop*, right out onto my head. I couldn't see ears under the mop of greasy, matted hair, hair that also grew over most of the giant's neck, though not on his face.

Around his shoulders, the giant wore a cape of hundreds, maybe thousands of animal skins crudely sewn together with stitches big enough to be seen a mile away. His torso was bare, not a pleasant sight, because the giant's breasts hung loose and in folds, lay flat against his grizzled paunch of a stomach.

Around his hips he wore another massive, pieced-together wrap of animal skins. For which I was seriously glad. I did not want to have to look at whatever was hiding underneath.

His feet were bare, hairy, and three-toed. It looked as if the two smaller toes on each foot had rotted off, leaving open, oozing sores. His hands looked no better, like the guy was suffering from leprosy. Which might have explained his missing nose and lips.

And did I mention that he could crush me between two of his existing fingers before I could say a word.

In the time it took me to get the full horror of the giant he stood still, shifting his mismatched eyes slowly from one of us to the next. But he made no other move.

"Uh, David?" Christopher squeaked. "What do we do now?"

Up to me, always up to me. Okay, couldn't get back into the diving bell. Even if we all made it in we'd be trapped, plucked out of the water like a miniature beach ball. Couldn't run for the water, swim away. One step and the giant could make it miles out, away from shore. We'd drown one way or another and we'd had enough of that. Try to rush past him, scatter, five bugs skittering along the floor, too many for the guy to focus on one? Assuming he was dumb. Assuming he wanted to focus on us. Assuming . . .

April screamed. With incredible speed for something so mammoth and deformed, the giant reached down with one disgusting hand for April.

I ran, holding the sword over my head with two hands, yelling at the top of my lungs, and brought the sword down on the giant's thumb as hard as I could, with as much fury as I could. The sword broke the skin, sliced into the bone, got stuck. Still the hand moved closer to April and I sawed and hacked and April, terrified, backed closer, closer to the lapping waves of the shore. I was vaguely aware of the fact that I was still roaring, that now Jalil and Christopher were roaring, too, and pelting the giant with stones and shells and basically doing nothing except pissing off the enemy.

Suddenly, the giant grunted and shook off me and my sword like the tiny nuisances we were. I fell on my butt, saw April charge down the beach, didn't see Senna. Saw Jalil back off a bit, run around behind me to help me up. Saw Christopher for some inexplicable reason continuing to taunt the giant with cries and whoops and yells, poking at the giant's foot with a sharp stick. Was he trying to distract him so I could get up to attack again, so April could get away?

"Christopher!" I shouted, on my feet. "Get out of the way!"

I raised the sword above my head just as the giant reached down again with his bloody hand, grabbed Christopher, and before I could take one step, put Christopher into his mouth.

EVER WORLD

#XI
MYSTIFY THE MAGICIAN

The sun came up watery and mist-filtered on a far busier scene. Old Lorg was still dead. But now the king had come with a type of guys we'd met in passing a long time before and a long way away: Fianna.

The Fianna, as I understood it, were knights of a sort, though they didn't go in for the whole shining-armor thing. They were the personal army of the High King. I figured the High King was like the president, with King Camulos being a governor. King Cam's fairies were the state troopers, the Fianna were the FBI and the Marines all rolled into one.

The Fiannans were quiet and polite and respectful. They addressed everyone by their title, or else as "Sir" or "Lady." They'd ridden through the night in response to a telegram sent by the king and arrived from the distant capital. Their massive horses were wandering around the fields eating grass.

A bunch of druids had also showed up. We had blue druids and green druids and red druids. It was a druid convention, but not what a person might picture: they were old and young, male and female, snappy dressers or old slobs. The one thing they all seemed to have in common was an incredible lack of stupidity.

The blue druids spent quite a while going over the giant's already fragrant body, poking, probing, and finally cutting. There was some discussion of dissecting Lorg — dissection was all the rage with blue druids — but no one had invented the chain saw yet, so it was hard to see how they were going to carve him up.

Still, they used handy scalpels and lancets and clunky, ornate tweezers, and pretty soon they had removed his canned ham of an eye and collected half a dozen bullets.

Jalil was busy being cross-examined by Fios, the only yellow druid there. I was hearing words like "firing pin" and "barrel" and "magazine." Fios was nodding his head like a psychiatrist who has just heard your sickest fantasy but doesn't want to act too grossed-out. Jalil looked embarrassed.

One of the blue druids, a chubby, grand-motherly woman, came over to me carrying a pottery jar with six bloody lumps rolling around inside.

"What are these called?" she asked me.

"Those are slugs. They're made of lead. Mostly, anyway. I guess there's copper, too. The copper holds them together a little, but see, the head of the slug still spreads out, mashes up, when it hits."

Grandma Druid gave me a funny look. "How does lead come to flatten thus? Even lead, softest of metals, is harder than flesh."

"Well, it's going very fast. Faster than an arrow. I mean, a lot faster. It hits and . . . *wham*. The lead flattens and then it tears through the muscle or whatever and . . ." I was performing helpful hand-gestures to illustrate.

You know, I'd have been happy to explain bullets to Ka Anor. Or Loki. Or Hel. Or Neptune. I'd have been happy to explain bullets in the most direct, hands-on way I could, but having to stand there and explain how a bullet tore through flesh and muscle and organs, explain all that to these decent-seeming people, that wasn't easy. Hard not to feel responsible.

"Ah," she said, and rolled the slugs back and forth.

Just then a fairy came zooming in to report to the king. They'd found a small boat floating just off-shore. A fishing boat, abandoned. And on the shore, wedged into the rocks, two dead fishermen who bore the same puncture wounds found in Lorg.

David had rounded up Jalil and April and gathered me up and the four of us stepped off a way from the crime-scene crowd.

"Someone's got a machine gun," David said in a low voice.

"Do you think so, McGarrett?" I said. "What gave it away?"

He clenched his jaw and looked like he wanted to hit me and only just restrained himself.

"We're kind of deep in it, here," David snapped. "Maybe not the time for sarcasm. None of these people is a fool: They're thinking we're responsible somehow."

Jalil shook his head. "No. We've given the Coo-Hatch some technology to make cannons. But from muzzle-loading cannons to full-auto weapons, that's a couple centuries."

"Senna's behind this," I said suddenly.

David's head snapped up, angry. "Don't say things like that. You want them to hear?"

"You know he's right," April said. "You know it's her. Otherwise why is it the four of us here talking and not Senna? You left her out, David. Why is that?"

I said, "I saw her, I was watching her when Jalil started talking about guns. Not a flicker. She didn't jerk guilty, but she didn't jerk surprised, either."

The four of us turned slowly and stared at Senna. She stood off by herself, pacing very slowly, looking as if she was taking a slow-motion tour of the stone walls. Deep in thought.

I noticed the head Fiannan, a guy with the excellent name of MacCool. He was watching us and watching our faces as we looked at Senna. It was a "cop" look.

I looked back at Senna. She was gone, hidden by some wafting mist.

MacCool wasn't so sure.

"The witch," he said loudly. "Where is the witch?"

A breeze blew the mist away. No Senna.

Fairies erupted into a blur, racing here and there, fanning out. The Fiannans spread out a bit more slowly than the fairies.

April left us and walked straight to Etain. She grabbed her arm.

David yelled, "April!"

Too late. "She's a shapeshifter," April said. "She could be anyone."

Etain nodded. "MacCool! The witch can change shape." Etain came striding over to us, suspicious, furious at everyone except April. "You should have warned me."

"She's one of us," David shot back.

"The hell she is," said Jalil.

"We came here together!" David yelled, suddenly almost out-of-control. "We came here together, we leave together, all of us, her too!"

I said, "We didn't come here, General, we were dragged. By her." To Etain I said, "We lied to you last night. We're here because Senna dragged us here. She's some kind of gateway between the old world and Everworld and she's also a freaking nut. She's got a power jones. She wants to be the newer, better Ka Anor. We've been her little sock puppets all along."

April joined in. "She's completely ruthless. And she has powers. More power all the time." She looked right at David. "Don't let her touch any of your people, Etain. That's how she's strongest."

"Why not just tell them to shoot on sight?" David demanded.

I said, "David, she's an evil bitch who sells us out any time it suits her. We're supposed to be loyal? To her?"

"We stick together!" David almost screamed. "I

know it looks bad. I know . . . but we stick together, man, that's the thing."

Jalil stepped close to David, got right in his face. "David, there's someone over here running around with a damned Uzi. And we all know somehow she's behind it."

Then suddenly Jalil grabbed David's arms, not like he was trying to control him, more like he was trying to hold himself up. Like someone had sucked the air out of his lungs and he needed to hold on or faint.

"What is it?" April asked.

"That's what she's going to do," Jalil said in a whisper. "That's what she's going to do. A gateway goes both ways. Of course. Oh, Jesus."

"Shut up, Jalil," David said, but there was no conviction behind it.

Jalil looked horrified, stared at David. "You guessed! You knew?"

David was wringing his hands, saying, "Just shut up, Jalil." As messed up as I have ever seen David. He looked like someone was piling bricks on his shoulders, like some growing weight was crushing him slowly down.

"David, you poor dumb son of a —"

I lost patience at the same moment as April. "What?" we both yelled. "What?"

Jalil wiped his face with his hand, wiped off

the sweat and the fog condensation. "You open a door between universes, who's to say which way the traffic flows?"

"Did you find that in a fortune cookie?"

"Senna won't let anyone use her. She wants power. She's not going to be Loki's tool, or anyone's tool. She's the gateway, she knows that. But it's not about whether she's going to let Loki and the others escape into the Real World. The traffic's going the other way, man. She's bringing people here. She's bringing them here. Men with guns."

It was a moment of crystalline revelation. It took my breath away. I laughed. Of course!

Senna was in a bind: If Merlin caught her she'd be locked away in his tower forever. If Loki caught her she'd be forced to become his gateway, open an escape route to the real world.

Neither choice exactly worked for Senna. Senna wanted it all. She knew her own magic was nowhere near powerful enough to make her a player in Everworld. Ah, but Senna with an army, an army with real-world weapons, that was a different story.

Lorg the giant was dead. The perfect symbol: Everworld's Goliath versus a real world David carrying an Uzi slingshot. Bye-bye Goliath.

* * *

We horsed up and headed back eventually to the town and King Cam's castle. All of us together, leaving behind some of the Fianna and a number of fairies. But MacCool rode with us. Rode right next to Etain as a matter of fact. Right up alongside her.

And that really should not have been tippy-top of my brain right then, what with all that had happened, what with the fact that Senna had escaped, but the brain and the body do what they want to do. Specially when the brain gets together with the body.

It's like the body is the bad friend your mom doesn't want you to hang around with, because man, however good your brain wants to be, however many promises old Brainiac makes, body can always bring him over to the dark side of the force.

Body was having a Harlequin kind of morning. Brain was trying real hard to be serious and focus on the fact that good old Senna had come up and kicked the chess board all over the place so that all of a sudden no one could remember where the pieces had been before. But Body was mainlining testosterone and looking to find some friendly estrogen. The Y chromosome wanted to go say "hi!" to the double X's. Body had its own separate memory of Etain's nightgown. And Body had been strangely excited by Etain's cool sword trick. Brain never had a chance.

And the thing was that MacCool was putting the moves on Etain. Not that she'd notice, naturally: Girls are always prepared to believe that a guy has something else in mind. Despite roughly a million years of human experience, females persist in their belief that deep down inside, guys are girls.

No doubt MacCool was talking about the killing. No doubt he was very professional. He looked like that kind of guy. But he was a hound, I had no doubt. He was giving her the thoughtful look, the considering nod, the old leaning-close-to-hear-better-while-inspecting-cleavage move.

I decided to demonstrate my maturity by pouting. Fine. Forget her. There were plenty more beautiful half-elf maidens who would jump at the chance to hook up with a penniless, cowardly minstrel from another universe.

My horse wasn't fast and I wasn't interested in pushing him. So my horse moseyed and stopped to munch, and I moseyed and pouted and wondered whether it really was just coincidence that Etain had come personally to my room.

I was at the back of the column, back behind the afterguard of Fianna and fairies. Just me and some sleepy, yawning, uniformed guys from the palace, and one of the Fianna, one of MacCool's boys leading a lame horse.

We came to a curve in the path as it went around a stand of trees, the three of us were bringing up the rear, and temporarily blocked from the view of the King and MacCool and Etain and David and the rest of the Important People.

The Fiannan decided to give up on keeping pace with his lame horse. He sighed and yanked his horse around and started back down the road from the direction we'd come. Taking the lame horse back to . . .

Back to what? Why not lead the horse on to the village?

I looked back just before I'd have lost sight of him entirely. And that's when I saw him abandon his horse and climb over a stone fence.

I knew right away. I knew it cold: it was Senna.

What I should do is race up the path, alert the King who'd send MacCool pelting back after her. And if MacCool or the fairies caught her I'd get a nice pat on the head.

I could see that scene, clear as day: MacCool with a sullen Senna in tow, my trotting along yelping, "I saw her! I saw her! I'm the one who saw her!"

Yeah. That would have Etain throwing Mac-Cool aside in favor of me. Cause if there's one thing a woman admires, it's a guy who can call for the help of a real man.

I reined in my horse. The sleepy uniformed guy kept going, and I thought for a second of telling him what I was doing, but no, he'd just go grab MacCool.

Screw MacCool.

I turned my horse. I could do this. I had a horse, Senna was on foot. Besides, I knew she'd be tired. We knew that about her, that doing the magic thing wore her out. She must have been shapeshifting for half an hour, at least, and she'd be beat. Sometimes the tiredness put her under, unconscious.

"Come on, Christopher. You're not scared of Senna," I told myself. But here's the thing: Any time you have to deny that you're scared, you're scared.

"It's just Senna," I told myself. "It's not like she's a troll, or a god or something really nasty."

No, it was just good old Senna. I had dated her. I'd kissed her. Of course that was before I'd seen her literally shift the course of an entire river.

"Man, you're meat," I told myself.

I couldn't see Senna any more. There were widely spaced trees and a slight up-slope. Maybe she was back in the trees. Maybe she was over the rise. Maybe she was asleep. Maybe she was gone altogether.

I had no weapon. But now I was in it, I couldn't wimp out. So I urged my horse to jump the stone fence. He didn't exactly jump. More like stumbled. We kicked over some rocks and the horse complained, although not in English, which was a relief.

I urged my horse onward and began searching desperately for a big stick, anything I could use as a weapon. I told myself that if I screamed the fairies would be all over us in a few seconds, but I didn't believe it. The fairies were fast but they weren't everywhere at once. And by now the King and Etain and my friends were all ten minutes further down the path. Didn't they even notice I wasn't there? I mean, if they all came riding back after me and arrived just as I found Senna, hey, I'd get full credit for being brave and for catching the witch. I'd be content with that. I'd have the intention of bravery, that was as good as actual bravery.

I topped the rise, leaning forward over the horse's neck to stay on in the slope. On the other side was a dell, I guess that's what you'd call it. A sort of shallow dimple in the land, maybe a hundred feet across, grassy in most places, more sparse under the gloomy trees.

In the center of the dell was a circle of crudely-cut stone pillars the size of upended Land Cruisers. Twelve in all, and each topped with a precariously balanced stone about big enough to eat dinner off of.

There in the center of the circle, shining through the mist, stood Senna.

I felt a chill go right through me. It was damp, and it was cold, and I was tired, but none of that was the reason for the chill.

She was very calm, waiting, not exactly relaxed, but not ready to go Jackie Chan on me, either. I reined-in well outside the circle of stones.

"Druid stones, like Stonehenge," Senna said conversationally, like I'd asked her a question. "They seem to have advanced quite a way since the days when they used these kinds of circles to plot the stars and the moon and regulate the planting days and the holidays and the harvests."

"Yeah," I said, dry-mouthed. "They have calendars now, I guess. Probably those Tolkien calendars. You know . . . like . . . okay."

"What am I supposed to do with you, Christopher?" Senna asked, cocking her head to one side.

"Come back with me," I said as firmly as I could.

She smiled and shook her head regretfully. "I don't think so, Christopher. These folks are simple, but not stupid. They know that what happened to Lorg wasn't magic. They know we're involved in some way. And you or Jalil or April would have sold me out to them."

I could deny it, but what would be the point? "Yeah. Not me, though. Not that I wouldn't, it's just that I would never have had a chance: It would be a toss-up between Jalil and April. Me, I don't like you, don't trust you, but I don't have a major beef with you."

She nodded, accepting that. "I wish I could trust you, Christopher, I really do."

"Can I kill him now?" a voice asked.

That voice . . . familiar. From somewhere, not here, but from somewhere. I looked around, saw no one. Just the stones, the trees, the grass.

"Yes, you can kill him now."

Keith loomed up from atop one of the massive rocks, rising to his full, not-very-impressive height. He cradled an Uzi in the crook of one arm. There was a pair of pistols holstered around his waist. An ammo belt hung over one shoulder.

Keith, the sick little racist Nazi-wannabe punk who had threatened me over in the real world. I didn't pause to wonder how in hell he'd ended up here, now, I just moved. Kicked my horse hard with both heels and rolled backward off him. Bang onto my back, thank God for soft grass, and still the wind was kicked out of me.

The Uzi erupted and the horse screamed. The

horse hit the ground, kicked, then stopped kick-ing.

I rolled up against the base of the nearest stone pillar. Tried to think. Keith. With a freaking Uzi. A little Klebold-Harris psychopath working with Senna. And me with nothing but handfuls of grass.

I heard Keith above. He was leaping from stone table to stone table. Leaping heavily. He was weighed down with all that hardware, not like me, no boy, thank goodness I had nothing to contend with but empty freaking hands. If I ran for the trees he'd have a perfect, easy shot at me. If I stayed in the stones he'd have a harder time, but there was Senna to deal with.

All I had survived in Everworld and I was going to get shot? Shot? With a gun?

THERE IS A PLACE THAT SHOULDN'T EXIST.
But does.

#1 SEARCH FOR SENNA
#2 LAND OF LOSS
#3 ENTER THE ENCHANTED
#4 REALM OF THE REAPER
#5 DISCOVER THE DESTROYER
#6 FEAR THE FANTASTIC
#7 GATEWAY TO THE GODS
#8 BRAVE THE BETRAYAL
#9 INSIDE THE ILLUSION
#10 UNDERSTAND THE UNKNOWN
#11 MYSTIFY THE MAGICIAN

Available wherever you buy books, or use this order form.